UW Library BOOK SALE

77 Best Canadian Stories

To read nearly all the literary magazines published in Canada during one year is to realize how ephemeral much of the work is and how precarious the lives of the magazines themselves. Most of the magazines have a very small circulation, 1500 copies being about the largest. Yet it is these magazines and the dedication of their editors which have traditionally fostered new talent and continue to do so.

In the past, the literary magazines were the proving ground of talent, a recognized stage of apprenticeship before the writer moved on to the master work of books. This is less true now than formerly. Most publishers are unwilling to even consider collections of short stories. The audience for serious writing is shrinking. Even established writers are happy to continue publishing in literary magazines with small circulations for nominal payment; they have little choice. This is as true of the United States and England as it is of Canada.

An anthology such as this offers some slight hope. It offers to a larger audience work that otherwise might well not have been seen; it extends the life of a piece of work; it directs the attention of readers to writers who otherwise might have been consigned to the vaults on microfilm.

The editorial task is not merely one of compilation; it is also critical. Frank Kermode described literary criticism as "the medium in which past work survives." We hope that this anthology and succeeding ones will serve this function as well as offering immediate pleasure.

JOAN HARCOURT/JOHN METCALF

The following magazines were consulted: *Antigonish Review, Canadian Fiction Magazine, Canadian Forum, Canadian Review, Capilano Review, Dalhousie Review, Exile, Fiddlehead, Grain, Impulse, Jewish Dialogue, Journal of*

Canadian Fiction, Malahat Review, Northern Journey, Ontario Review, Prism International, Quarry, Queen's Quarterly, Saturday Night, Tamarack Review, University of Windsor Review, Wascana Review, West Coast Review.

Acknowledgements: "Illianna Comes Home" by W. P. Kinsella is reprinted from *Canadian Fiction Magazine*; "Trees" by W. D. Valgardson from *The Ontario Review*. An earlier version of "Travelling On" by Beth Harvor appeared in the *Journal of Canadian Fiction* under the title "Stars, Moons" and an earlier version of "More than Conquerors" by Jack Hodgins was published in the same magazine. "Prelude to a Parking Lot" by Elizabeth Spencer is reprinted from *Southern Review*; "At Peace" by Ann Copeland from *Canadian Fiction Magazine*. "Cuixmala" by Judith Penner is previously unpublished. "Perhaps the Church Building Itself" by Kent Thompson was broadcast on CBC *Anthology*. The editors' special thanks to Robert Weaver and Howard Engel for making available to them stories broadcast on CBC *Anthology*.

Contributions for the eighth volume, published or unpublished, should be sent to the editors at Box 1061, Kingston, Ontario, or Box 220, Delta, Ontario, before 30 November, 1977.

Publishers of literary magazines who would like to have their stories considered are invited to send current issues to the editors at either of the box numbers above.

Illianna Comes Home

W. P. Kinsella

My name is Silas Ermineskin. I am eighteen years old. Me and Frank Fence-post and a couple of other guys are taking a course that the government offers on how to be mechanics. I fix things pretty good and our instructor, Mr. Nichols, say he think he can get me an apprentice job with a tractor company in Wetaskiwin when I finish.

One part of the course I don't like is that I got to write an essay. I'm lucky I can write. Frank Fence-post can write most of his name, but he is faking everything else since the course started. Mr. Nichols says I got a funny sense of humour, so I should just write about the funniest thing that ever happened to me.

I been thinking about that, and I think the funniest thing that ever happened to me was when my sister Illianna came home to the reserve with her white man husband.

Illianna she smart. She stayed at school until grade eight and then went all the way to Calgary to work. She worked too. Waited tables at the New Zenith Café and she don't drink and do bad things like Suzie Calf-robe and some of the other girls who go to the city. Illianna she pretty, and she proud she pretty. She say to me in one of her letters she not going to do nothing to spoil herself, like drink and fight.

Eathen Firstrider he sure is mad when she up and goes

away, because he been her boyfriend ever since she was twelve, and he figure they would get married. Eathen he won $50 in the calf-roping contest at the Ponoka Stampede last summer. When he do, he buy a record of Buffy St. Marie, even though he ain't got no record player, because he say she look like Illianna. He got the record picture on the wall of his cabin. He still figures that he gonna marry with Illianna some day.

Then Illianna writes home that she married with a white man. Mrs. Robert McGregor McVey is what we should call her now. Her husband is a businessman. He's old too, 25, and even been for one year to the university somewhere. Illianna she don't work no more and they got an apartment in one of the big buildings in Calgary.

Ma, she has bad feelings that our Illianna married with a white man. But she not half as mad as Eathen Firstrider when I tell him. Eathen, he polishes the big blade of his hunting knife on his jeans and talks about taking scalps. Frank Fence-post, he laugh and say, "We don't do that no more."

"It's time we started again," says Eathen. Then he throws the knife right through the one-by-four side of the kindling box. Eathen he's already twenty and all us guys look up to him. He rides in the rodeos and knows all about girls and cars. Two years ago he was outrider on the chuckwagon races at the Calgary Stampede. He spent $25 of his wages on a white girl down at the Queen's Hotel, and she taught him all kinds of things that he wasn't too sure about. When he got back he told us guys about it for two hours and how he was gonna do all these things to and with Illianna. And he weren't lying to us. He don't know, but me and Frank and Charlie Fence-post was hanging off the roof of the cabin looking in the window.

Eathen sure figured that he was going to marry Illianna,

but it wasn't long until she went away to Calgary. Eathen still figures all them things he taught her made her able to catch a white man, and he gets mad every time he think about it. But I bet Illianna being tall and slim and pretty helped some too.

Anyway, Illianna was married a year when she say in a letter she coming home for a long weekend with her white man husband.

They pull into the yard in a new car, one with chrome wheels and white and blue racing stripes. A car so big and new that it looks like it belong to a finance man.

The car stops and the kids come creeping out from behind the cabins like the deer do sometimes when they think there is no-one around. The kids walk with their necks out and like they haven't got any toes. Eathen Firstrider is standing cross-legged against the wall of his cabin, smoking a roll-yer-own that is about as long and thin as he is.

If Illianna wasn't my sister, I wouldn't have known her. She let her hair grow real long and she be wearing a white coat, a white suit, and white boots. I think while I'm walking up to her that Illianna, she going to be a white woman one way or another.

Then her husband, he get out, and he look like one of them pictures out of the Eaton's catalogue. He got a hat with a funny little brim, an overcoat, and a suit and tie. He got shiny black shoes with toe rubbers too.

He shake hands with me, and Ma too. Ma ignores him, and she don't speak so much on Illianna. Ma's wearing her good speckled dress and her purple kerchief. She looks in the back of the car, not walking over to it but just by rolling her eyes. Then she looks hard on Illianna's tummy and say, "Where your babies?"

"Ma," Illianna say, giving her a real harsh look.

"Well, where your babies?"

9

"We haven't got any babies."

"How come? You been married most a year. When I been married a year I had you and Joseph already, and Silas in my stomach."

"Really Ma. We just don't want children yet." Illianna, by her voice lets Ma know she wishes she would shut up. Ma just nods knowingly and continues right on.

"What's with don't want? You get a good man you get lots of babies. What's wrong with him?" She nods toward McVey who has been standing like he frozen, one hand still stuck out in front like maybe he going to shake hands on someone else. About this time Eathen Firstrider strolls across the yard, walking very slow.

"Hello Illianna," he says. Then he say some very personal things to her in our language. Now I know why Ma and Eathen have been holding council in our cabin for the last three days. That white man, he'd take his hand back quick if he knew what Eathen was saying. Illianna's cheeks get bright pink and she looks sharp on her McVey, but he is not interested in Eathen.

McVey has moved in on Ma, and he is trying to make himself useful by explaining his financial position and telling her that it will be two more years before they can afford babies. He assures Ma that Illianna and him will have kids when they want them, only I'm sure I hear him say something about papooses. Ma she just look blank and roll her eyes like when she have too much moonshine. Illianna she got one hand on McVey's sleeve kind of pulling him back, but she listening too, only to Eathen Firstrider, who say things that make everyone blush, except McVey, who don't know anyone but him is talking.

When McVey stops for breath, Ma, she just goes on from where she left off before.

"Louis Coyote, he blind," she say, "he lost his leg when

the tractor run over him, but he still make babies. Edith Coyote pop any day now with their fifteenth."

McVey he just kind of shake his head, then he explain things to Ma again. Only this time he tells it like he was talking to a little kid. When he is finished Ma speaks in our language to Illianna.

"What's she say?" McVey asks Illianna.

"She wants me to tell her what you said."

"But you said she understands English. . ."

Ma interrupted him again to speak to Illianna.

"She says she only understands English when an Indian speaks it," says Illianna.

"That's impossible," says McVey, who is about a foot shorter than Eathen, even with his fancy hat on.

"I'm sorry, Bob," Illianna says, "let's go inside. I'll have a talk with Ma later." Then she gives Eathen a funny smile, and me the same, like she was saying the thing for her to do was get into the fancy car and drive back to the city. Instead, we all go into the cabin where Ma is mumbling in our language about, "Money don't have nothing to do with make babies."

"I'll bring in your suitcase," I say to McVey.

He looks hard on Illianna, but she smiles on me.

"That would be very nice, Silas," she says.

McVey gives me the keys to his car, but very slowly like it is part of his hand he is passing to me.

"You be careful you don't scratch nothing, Si," he says to me. Si, I ain't never been called Si in my whole life.

There must be fifteen kids gathered around the car with their faces pressed against the windows. They are just looking at the white upholstery and touching the shiny paint. Frank Fence-post is there running the aerial up and down. I get the suitcase out of the back seat and one of the younger kids lugs it into the cabin. My girlfriend, Sadie One-wound has arrived.

"Boy, that's some big car," she says, "Will you buy us one like this when you get a job?"

"First pay cheque," I promise.

"Can I sit in it, Silas?"

"Well, I don't know." But Frank already has the door open and about a dozen kids are climbing in the back. I get behind the wheel, just to keep Frank from sitting there, and Sadie crawls over me and squeezes in next to Frank. Margaret Standing-at-the-door has just crawled through the passenger window and is sitting on Frank's lap.

"Start it up," yells Sadie, and the kids in the back cheer. I figure it won't do no harm to start the motor, so I give the key a turn and boy do it ever start fast.

Up to this time I ain't drove so much. I used to sit in the One-wound's Studebaker with no wheels and shift gears until the finance men came and towed it away.

About ten seconds after I start the car my brother-in-law charges out of the cabin, and he's coming for me with a not nice look on his face.

"Get going," yells Frank. Then he pulls the gear-shift into drive, reaches over and stomps my foot on the gas pedal so hard that the car nearly stands on its hind legs. The car sprays dirt and gravel and from the terrible yell I hear, I guess that McVey was behind the car. We shoot straight ahead, miss the corner of One-wound's cabin by only a little bit, and lose Charlie Fence-post who was too late to get in the car, but was sitting on the hood.

"Steer," yells Sadie above everyone else. But I just watch what is happening, which is when we drive over part of an old land disc, a tire goes bang and we swing to the left and straight into the slough behind Wolfchild's cabin. V-room, v-room, the car goes, and shoots mud and water back a long way, which is far enough to spray McVey and Charlie Fence-post who are coming after us. The kids in the back are all cheering. Sadie One-wound hugs my arm, and the car still goes v-room, v-room.

McVey runs into the water, opens the door and pulls out the keys. He uses cuss words on me that I never heard before, so I guess there are still things that we can learn from the white man. Me and Frank are busy saying how we'll get Louis Coyote's pickup and pull the car right out. McVey is busy clearing the kids out of the back of the car and telling me to shut to hell up, and he'll call the AMA, whatever that is. I hope it ain't nothing to do with the RCMP.

It turns out that the AMA is the tow truck up at Wetaskiwin, which is about eleven miles away. McVey he say he don't need no help from us, but after he walks all the way to Hobbema Crossing to use the phone at the service station, with us and the little kids walking a respectable distance behind him, it seems that the tow truck won't come out to the reserve for nobody no matter how white he is. So we all go and get Louis Coyote's pickup and with McVey directing, pull the car out and change the tire. Illianna is really mad with us, because mainly of McVey's suit which she say cost $200, and the fact, she says, that he catches cold so easy.

We all try to talk soft on him after that. I take him for a walk around the reserve, along the way we pick up the Fence-post boys and a few others. I show him my collection of car parts. Frank, he talks lots about how we strip down cars when we know the finance men coming to take them away, and how we changed plates and painted Louis Coyote's pickup so that even the finance men don't know it no more.

"It been most a year since anyone been looking for that truck," says Frank, and tells about how when we hear the finance men is coming we quick tear up the culvert by the slough so they got to walk instead of drive around the reserve.

"I am employed by a finance company," says my brother-in-law.

"Hey, partner, I been lying to you," says Frank thinking real fast.

McVey gives us a talk like they do down to the technical school, and he use the same voice he used on Ma a while ago. He tells us how it's not nice to strip down cars and trucks and how other people have to pay for it when we do things like that, and how if we'd only pay our bills there wouldn't be no trouble.

Frank, he say it sure is nice for them other people to pay and all, because he always been worried that the RCMP come around looking for something else but moonshine. Brother Bob he just shake his head and kick little rocks with his toe rubbers.

"You think we should let him get away?" Frank says to me in our language. "You can bet the finance man's gonna come back after Louis' pickup, and maybe even the RCMP after our car parts."

"We could drown him over in Muskrat Lake," says Charlie Fence-post. "Illianna, she don't miss him after a couple of days, and I bet nobody else would."

"Or we could just sort of lose him, leave him out in the dark for Eathen Firstrider to find," says Frank.

"I have a better idea," I say. "We don't do nothing to him. Ma and Mad Etta and Eathen, they got something planned. Better we shouldn't do nothing to upset it."

"What are you guys talking about," says McVey.

"We sure do like your little rubber shoes, partner," Frank tells him.

It sure is bad that McVey should be a finance man. This makes him to us like the cavalry must have been to the old time Indian. He is also like magpie, whenever his mouth open bad sounds come out. When I tell him my girlfriend

Sadie One-wound has fifteen brothers and sisters, McVey, he say with a laugh, "No wonder they call you guys fucking Indians." No-one laugh and McVey he sure wish he is back in the big city.

Ma been holding council with Mad Etta over to her cabin. Mad Etta is sort of our medicine man. She is so big she got a tree-trunk chair over at her cabin, because ordinary chairs crack up when she sits on them. I've seen them bulldog smaller steers at the rodeos. Everyone know that over at the Alice Hotel in Wetaskiwin, they got two chairs wired together and braced with two-by-fours so Mad Etta can drink beer and not bust up the furniture.

It is next morning before we find out what Ma and Mad Etta are planning. The night before, we give Illianna and her husband the other bed in the cabin, so me and the kids sleep on the floor. I lie awake and listen while Illianna teases McVey in a nice way, about they should try to make a baby.

"Good God, no," says McVey, "why there must be ten other people all around us."

Illianna laugh her pretty laugh and say that they won't hear nothing that they haven't heard before. And I bet she thinking of the fun she used to have with Eathen Firstrider back when she lived here and that used to be her bed.

I can tell by the way the cabin creaks that Frank Fence-post is on the roof, hanging over the edge and looking in on Illianna and her white man. He may as well go to sleep like I do.

At breakfast, Ma talks away in our language.

"You got to get *him* out for the evening, me and Mad Etta and somebody else we got a nice surprise for Illianna." By her tone of voice nobody would know she wasn't talking about the porridge she is stirring up. The *him* she talks about is of course McVey, but she refer to him in our language as, "he who has no balls."

Illianna lights into Ma after that, and McVey must figure nobody speaks English no more as he sits polishing his spoon and knife on his tie.

Ma, she don't back away one bit. What she says to Illianna is pretty hard to make into English but it amount to, "You may love your white man for the fancy things he can give you but you still got hot pants for Eathen Firstrider."

Illianna, she laugh and throw up her hands. Then she say to McVey in English, "You wear your warm coat today. You know how easy you take cold."

After breakfast, I say to McVey, "Brother Bob, we is really sorry about what we do to the car and for all the trouble we cause. We want you should enjoy your visit here, so tonight me and Frank and some of the boys, we make party for you. Show you good time. We going to make you an honourary Indian, just like when the Premier come down here to get us to vote for him."

You had better believe that I had to do some tall talking to get the boys to agree to that. I say, "Look, we make him a blood brother, he won't go sending the other finance men snooping around here and he don't send the RCMP after our car parts. It a lot better than killing him. Besides, I think he would like to be nice to us but he don't know how."

"We should drown him in Muskrat Lake," says Frank Fence-post.

McVey look at me up and down like maybe I want to borrow money from him. Then he say he guesses it would be okay we have the party. We say fine, and start to make plans that we take him to the ceremonial clearing which is way back in the hills a half mile, and which we just decide is going to be ceremonial clearing.

We send Frank Fence-post down to the Chief's cabin to borrow the ceremonial war bonnet, the same one we tie on the Premier and some French hockey player who claimed he was a quarter Assinoboine. But word travels fast on the reserve and the Chief he say among other things no white finance man ever going to wear the tribal war bonnet. So instead of war bonnet, Frank he come back with a five gallon cream-can full of dandelion wine that he borrow without asking.

Most of the day McVey he stay pretty close to Illianna and to his fancy car. About supper time, me and the boys go over to Mad Etta's. She been three days boiling up some strong medicine for Eathen Firstrider. Mad Etta she make the medicine out of tiger lilies, paintbrush, pig bristles, and many things that only she know about. It smell so strong that it hurt my nose from outside the cabin. We have to make fun on Eathen so that he brave to go in. The medicine be boiling on the back of the stove in an open pan, and it look like an oil change down at the Texaco garage.

Eathen is now not nearly so brave or so tall as he has been.

"How I going to drink pig bristles?" he wants to know.

"You drink," say Mad Etta, "or Etta sit on you and make you drink."

We all make some more fun on Eathen so he has to drink or look like he afraid. So he drink.

"You make many babies now," says Mad Etta. "Anybody you lie down with have many babies, even Etta." Then she laugh and laugh, shaking on her tree-trunk chair.

"Etta could have babies and nobody would know," she say, and laugh and laugh, patting her five-flour-sack dress.

My girlfriend, Sadie One-wound stop me on the way home from Mad Etta's and wants to know who pulled most of the feathers out of the turkey that her father keeps in a pen behind their house. I don't know.

But I find out when all us guys get to the clearing about nine that evening. Frank and Charlie got a good fire going and they already been sampling the wine that they borrowed.

Frank, he got a long piece of paper with turkey feathers glued down each side, and he fasten this on Brother Bob's head as soon as we get there.

"We is sorry we can't get the tribal war bonnet from the Chief," he say, "but this we make ourselves."

"It's very nice," Brother Bob say, but he look around funny like maybe he wish he have some other finance men there to keep him company.

Frank gets a big water dipper full of wine and gives it to McVey.

"That don't taste like wine," my brother-in-law say, "it's too sweet."

"Plenty honey in it," says Frank.

"It's the frogs that give it the sweet taste," says Charlie.

Brother Bob kind of choke a little, but then he see that we are just making fun on him. McVey goes to put down the dipper, but Frank lifts his arm back up.

"You gonna be Indian, you drink like Indian."

So Brother Bob finishes the dipper and Frank fills it again.

"I didn't mean to say it wasn't good," he say, and he smile on us for the first time since he come home with Illianna.

Illianna make me promise to look after McVey and see that he don't catch no cold. I figure that plenty of wine keep him warm and also make him nice to know. We all know that home-made wine kick harder than bucking horse. But McVey he don't know that.

After a while we all have lots of wine and we make noises and dance around the way we think a white man would expect us to. Then we put our hands on his hands and name him Robert Fire-chief our blood brother. Fire-chief is a name that Frank got from down at the Hobbema Texaco garage.

Like I promised Illianna, I try to look after our new Indian, but after the wine starts him to glow, he runs around making what he thinks are war whoops, and singing "One Little, Two Little, Three Little Indians," and stomping around in a circle like a movie Indian.

McVey thinks that the name Fire-chief makes him a chief. So he lead us whooping around the clearing and then down the trail a ways. He is yelling something about Tonto and silver bullets. What he don't know is that we coming to a pretty deep creek. I remember what I promise Illianna and am just about to tell him watch out, when a little by himself and with a little help from Frank Fence-post he falls head first into the water. He come up looking like a calf in a mud hole.

He is one wet Indian. We herd him back to Wolfchild's cabin which is the closest one to where we are. He is sneezing already, and boy do I know Illianna is going to be mad on me. We set McVey on the floor in front of the stove which Frank and me is filling with cut pine. Then we dig up an old pair of Eddy Wolfchild's jeans and a shirt that belong to his sister.

"That's mighty white of you guys," say my brother-in-law.

While we are wiping off the mud and trying to warm up our new Indian, Charlie Fence-post comes running back from our cabin where he has gone to check on how Eathen is doing. He pull me off to one side.

"Eathen over there all right," he say, "but it no wonder she ain't got no babies. Even I know they don't get no babies from what they doing to each other."

"Give Eathen time," I say, "he got to do first all the tricks that white girl in Calgary showed him. Eathen he know how babies made, but with Mad Etta's medicine in him, he get babies any way he do it."

Edith Wolfchild comes home while we all sitting around. She look at Brother Bob shivering on the floor.

"You cold, huh?" she say to him, and then cuddles up close.

Frank Fence-post he makes a bad face, but I say pointing at McVey, "He blood brother now, if Edith likes him that's her business."

I don't think Edith so much likes McVey as she don't like Illianna, which is a long time story, so guess she figures to get even on Illianna for whatever wrong she done her. Edith puts her fat little arms around McVey and kisses him lots. He come to life and touch her back some. She lead him over to the bed and start taking off the clothes that we just put on him.

"Go away, you guys," she says to us, but we don't.

They get under the covers. Edith is do a lot of moving around, but I think I can hear Brother Bob's teeth still chattering. Before long Edith gets out of bed and starts putting on her clothes. McVey, looking very sick, wraps a blanket around himself and sits on the oven door. The cabin gets a little warm by now.

Eathen comes running into the cabin. He is about a foot taller than he was over at Mad Etta's, so I know without asking that all has gone pretty good over at our place. He smile a lot on Robert Fire-chief.

"We are blood brothers, now," he tells him a few times.

Eathen sure feels big to tell him this. Fire-chief just sits stupid on the oven door. He has eyes like a dead owl and burps a lot.

Next morning, McVey is very pale, even for a white man, very quiet and look some smaller than when he come. He also has a cold for which Illianna is very mad on me and the boys. Me and the Fence-post boys say good-bye to him in his Indian name and he seem some pleased.

"Fire-water plenty bad," he say, and try to laugh, but we can see it hurt his head to do that. Eathen saunters by and smile on Illianna. He tells Illianna personal things again.

"Next time you come bring lots of babies," says Ma.

They is all ready to go but the fancy car won't start. Mc-Vey look under the hood and wants to know who the hell took off with the distributor, but we all say we don't know much about cars, and maybe the kids been playing with it or something.

We borrow Louis Coyote's pickup again and drive them to catch the bus at Hobbema Crossing. Illianna she real quiet and look at us like we cow chips or something. McVey, he say Wounded Knee gonna look like a picnic when he gets through with us. I think he even say he gonna write his MP.

Next morning a whole string of cars come up the road into the reserve. There is the big white tow truck from Wetaskiwin, a car full of RCMP and about eight guys in suits and hats who look just like Brother Bob. They move right along and we barely have time to tear the culvert out by the slough so they have to walk up to the houses.

Eathen, he be with the fancy car, about eight miles back in the hills. It funny, but all of a sudden, today, none of us speak English very much. We never heard of anybody named Eathen Firstrider, and the Ermineskins all moved away a long time ago, to Calgary, maybe.

Cars? No, we ain't got no cars. One old pickup truck around sometimes, but it down to the rodeo at Drumheller for a week or so. They all finally go away shaking their heads and saying how dumb we are.

Illianna write to us to say we better send back the car or she never have anything to do with us again. But we know she don't stay mad with us forever.

She write again in a few months to say she gonna have a baby. You think that don't get a celebration. Me and Ma and Eathen borrow the truck, load Mad Etta in the back and go to Wetaskiwin. We set Etta on her two chairs together at the Alice Hotel and buy her lots of beer.

Illianna sends us a little white card when the baby come. A boy, they call him Robert Ermineskin McVey. He looks like Ma, say Illianna.

Everybody counts their fingers and sure enough it's within about a week of when she was home. We have another celebration. Everybody they shake hands with Eathen First-rider, and give drinks to Mad Etta. Everyone is very much proud that Illianna have an Indian baby.

All us guys learned to drive on the fancy car. It got the muffler torn off and pretty well shot to hell by now, but Eathen still drives everybody around the reserve in it.

I'm not so sure anymore that it is such a funny thing I have written about, but if it gets me a job with the tractor company, then I guess it's okay.

Trees

W. D. Valgardson

Esther regarded the walnut trees from her front porch. Her house, with its porch supported by four round pillars, its white walls and dark roof, was set on a rise. It was not a proper hill that lifted the frame building above the surrounding countryside—there were no hills here—but only a falling away of the ground to meadow and cultivated fields. Small as the difference in height was, she valued it, for it meant her view of the grove was unobstructed. In the clear light of morning, the trees made a soft, rounded island that floated, pale green, above the endless rows of brown milo.

In the pasture, her herd of Holsteins, their black-and-white skins gleaming like washed boulders, were resting, their heads all turned in the same direction so that they seemed to be intent on a person or happening which was hidden from her. Later, when the sun stood above the dark crest of the roof, hot and blinding as the open door of a furnace, the cows would awkwardly heave themselves up and amble toward the trees. In the dappled shade, they would studiously chew their cud. Later, expecting to be fed and cared for, they would file toward the house with the unhurried dignity of gods, certain of their rights and the obligations of others.

A faded black Oldsmobile shot from behind a screen of grey-green sumac and turned onto the quarter-mile of scraped dirt Esther called her private drive. The car stopped, the driver got out, unhooked her gate, swung it out of the way and, after driving through, left it hanging open.

If she had thought it would do any good, she would have waved at the driver to remind him to go back and close the gate. It was not that she feared her cows would wander onto the road—in the heat, an electric prod would barely force them to their feet—it was the lack of consideration that annoyed her. It was her gate and it had been built for the express purpose of being closed. For it to be left open seemed a slight.

If she had not already been seen, she would have ducked into the house and stayed in her bedroom until the car left again. Unable to escape the visit, she waited rigidly in her blue dress, her feet planted slightly apart, a hand pressed to one of the pillars, the other clenched on the shelf of her hip.

She was tall, with a pale angular quality that suggested obscured gentility. People who did not know her immediately thought she was a stranger to the district, a school teacher who had married a local farmer, for example, but she was not. She had been born here and lived here all her life except for the six months between the end of grade twelve and her father's first heart attack. She had gone to the city to study to be a secretary and still kept her typewriter and all her books on a desk in one corner of the living-room. Since her father's death, she had run the farm with the help of a hired man. At planting and harvest, her uncle came to assist with the crop.

Grey dust billowed skyward from the Oldsmobile and when the car, just before it seemed ready to crash into the corner of the house, jerked to a stop, the gritty cloud engulfed it so that, for a moment, it sat fixed and ominous, in the centre of its own storm. All at once, as if having expended its force, the dust drifted forward and settled over the porch. The driver's door was forced open and Ronald D. Reasner climbed out.

Ronald was a large, awkward youth with a shaved head. He wore a black shirt with a pink fish embroidered on the front, red slacks too short in the leg and scuffed cowboy boots. He looked foolish enough to be seventeen but he was closer to 30. He had, for a number of years, tried carpentering but had finally given it up to travel about the countryside on his father's business. He hurried around the car and opened the rear door.

First, Dominic's hat appeared. Brown, wide-brimmed, faded and stained, it hung limp as a frost-killed rhubarb leaf. He grasped the top of the door with one grimy hand and pulled himself out.

As a child, he had suffered from rickets and his softened bones had warped beneath his weight until they bent outward like drawn bows. Under normal circumstances, he would have been a tall man but his curved legs shortened him so that his head barely reached above the car roof. His son shut the door. Dominic did not try to walk any farther but leaned forward, both hands pressing down on his cane. His eyes were hidden by his hat.

"$40," he said.

"They're not for sale," she replied. She meant her voice to be quiet and firm but it caught in her throat and came out thin and high.

"$50. Half in advance, half when the job is done." Dominic's yellow chin jutted from under the shadow of his hat. He wore a threadbare brown suit which was too big for him. It had been someone else's and, to make it fit, he had cinched the pants so tightly at the waist that they were gathered like drapes.

Esther crossed her arms over her chest and stared over Dominic's hat. The trees were pale jade. Behind them, a thundercloud rose like an anvil in the sky.

"$2650," he said. "And I have some milking equipment and a storage tank I can let you have against what I'd pay you. It'll save you a trip to the city."

"They're not for sale," she repeated stubbornly.

"We need wood for the mill. If I don't get it, I got to lay somebody off."

"Cut somebody else's trees."

"Yours are all that's left. Everything worth cutting for 30 miles has been cut." His cane had been made by beating a brass doorknob onto a hawthorn stem. He clenched it fiercely, one hand clasped over the other. His fingers were the colour of newspaper left all summer in the sun.

The ground before the house was worn flat and hard as stone. Scraps of grass clung to the surface like bits of scattered cellophane. Ronald was polishing the fender mirror with his sleeve.

"The agricultural people were here yesterday. You've gotta have a cement floor and new equipment."

At last, he had revealed his reason for thinking he would be successful. To Esther, the porch seemed to grow smaller. In spite of the heat, she pulled her arms more tightly about her.

"They're not for sale."

He nodded his head slowly as though the movement cost him a great deal of effort.

"We can come anytime. You call my son. He'll take care of the details."

She did not move until the car was out of sight but then she grasped the closest pillar with her left hand. Dominic's coming had upset her. Instinctively, even before there was any outward sign, he could smell weakness. When disease or misfortune struck, he appeared, his profit already calculated.

He was, she told herself, nothing. He had nothing, he was nothing, he counted for nothing.

He was nothing but he sold everything—used furniture, seneca root, hides, sick cows, second-hand machinery, used clothing. Nobody knew much about him before he came to the district but there constantly were rumours. No-one had seen his wife but it was said that when she died, he sat her up in the back seat of his car and drove her to the city in the hope of selling her to the medical school.

Esther looked out over her property. It measured a mile in every direction, 640 acres. To walk the roads that bounded it took an hour. Except for the grove of walnut, every tree—sycamore, persimmon, catalpa—had all been rooted out, the ground ploughed over for pasture or planted in crops. At one time, there had been a lawn all the way to the county road, a thicket where she picked persimmons for jam, and a garden full of watermelon and pumpkins and okra but it was all gone now. The cattle left her no time for a garden so it had been turned over to milo and the lawn to pasture. The trees had been unproductive and, as well, they kept the ground around them from growing grain. She had not given over the farm to the caring of her dairy herd all at once, but rather, a little at a time as grain rose in price and cows became sick or the barn needed repairs.

Long before she had taken over the farm, Dominic had been after the trees. The day following her father's funeral, Dominic had approached her about them. She had sent him away.

The trees were, she told herself, an asset, providing her cows with a natural shelter and saving her from having to build a windbreak. They were money in the bank. Year after year, they grew in value. Each fall they provided a cash crop.

She had no time for picking the nuts herself but people drove out from town and gathered them. It was understood that she was to get half. Half for ownership, half for labour, a fair division. Except that most cheated her, hiding an extra bushel or two in their trunk and, as she abhorred scenes, she let them past the house without insisting on searching their vehicles. When the nuts were all picked, she had no more than a couple of hundred pounds. She shucked the green walnuts by laying them in the ruts of her lane. The weight of the truck as it went back and forth ripped the thick, green pulp away. After a rain or two, the shells were clean and ready for storing. On winter evenings, she cracked them and picked out the meats.

In spite of the heat and the clear sky above, she knew it would rain. The thundercloud was bigger. She watched it critically as though her disapproval would drive it back. She hoped it would not rain long. There was a lot of outside work to be done, and she could not afford to have her hired man leave.

Rain bothered his kidneys. So, for that matter, did sleet, snow, cold and heat. To help relieve sudden attacks of pain, he wore two flasks of homebrew in his hip pockets. He shambled through the seasons in a slow daze, disappearing and reappearing at irregular intervals. When he left, he never notified her. Her first hint was always that some piece of work was not done. When her father was alive, she kept the hired man on the back porch but once Esther was living alone, she had the tool shed done over and moved him into it. Whenever she became suspicious he had gone, she trudged close enough to his shack to see if there was a note tacked to the door. She did not have to read it. It was a much-crumpled, stained sheet with the message "Gone to my sister's for my kidneys" drawn in block letters.

He would lie in his sister's spare room, drying out, until

his sister could stand it no longer and drove him out with a broom. He would reappear without a hint of apology. Esther survived such episodes in quiet desperation, doing all she could and letting the non-essentials go. By the time her hired man came back, she was so tired that she did not have the energy to scold him.

As it was, she never seemed to catch up. The house had needed painting since before she had returned from the city. In her first year, when she was still possessed of seemingly endless energy, she had scraped the wall facing the road and had painted it white. There had been no time since to finish the job. The two one-gallon cans of paint were stored under her bed.

The house did not look neglected so much as it looked worn out. The boards seemed so thin that, on seeing them for the first time, a newcomer would have suspected that someone might be secretly rubbing them every night with emery. When Esther cut short her stay in Kansas City, she had been nineteen, plump and dimpled. Now, she was all angles and her fingers were so thin they might have been sharpened with pumice.

She had not expected to stay home for more than a month or two but her father's heart attacks, five in all, had kept her bound to the farm. Since his death, the mortgage and his medical bills had kept her from selling out. Still, she was resolved to return to the city eventually and was determined not to let her appearance go. She bought skin cream and bath oil through the mail. It had helped but it had not been enough. She had changed. The constant work and worry and dealing with those who were quick to take advantage of a woman living alone had tightened her face and made her eyes wary.

With the first drop of rain, she decided to go into town. She needed bread but, most of all, she needed to get away and talk to someone.

"Like a rat," Helga, the baker's wife said, referring to Dominic. "He never sleeps. Gathering. Gathering. They say his outbuildings are jammed so full of objects you can hardly get into them anymore." Her face, bright red from the heat of the ovens, pulled together in disapproval. "We tried to save money to go to Florida but he got it all for an oven he brought from the city. He knew we had to have it and if he brought it and showed it to us, we'd have no choice but to take it."

Condensation made the windows opaque. Esther wiped the glass clear with the side of her hand. Across the street, Dominic owned a red brick building that was 60 feet long and 50 feet wide. At one time, it had been divided into three parts and had housed a mortician, a café and a general store. He had used all of it for storage except the mortician's waiting room which he kept for an office. The waiting room had a large glass window and Dominic had positioned his desk so that when he was sitting behind it he could see the entire street. Nothing escaped his scrutiny.

His son had painted *Dominic D. Reasner Enterprises, Acquisitions and Sales* in gold. The walls of the office were lined with filing cabinets and the cabinets were filled with files on every object Dominic had ever bought or sold, or ever hoped to buy or sell. It made no difference whether you wanted 100 acres of land or a rake. He went directly to the proper file, drew his hand over the folders, then extracted the right sheets. No-one had ever seen him make a mistake. In a moment, he could review the entire history of the object and so calculate the price. If you ordered a new washing machine from the Sears' store and he heard about it, which he inevitably did, you could be assured that he began a new file with the date, the brand, how much you paid, how often you washed clothes, all in anticipation of the day you came to sell it or he came to buy it.

It was rumoured that in the locked cabinets against the back wall he kept files on every man, woman and child in the county, recording everything there was to know about them. Before he made a deal with anyone in which they could not pay cash or in which he was doing the buying, he sent them away so that he could study their history. At times, fear of the files had grown so great that men had talked of breaking into the office and stealing them. Nothing had ever come of it.

As she watched him, she was sure he had studied her file carefully. He knew her every sin, every weakness, every omission.

"A rat," the baker's wife said. "That's what he reminds me of. We've got a sewer in the basement and we used to keep it plugged with a thick wood lid. I kept worrying about a rat chewing its way in. One day I lifted it and the lid was gnawed nearly through." She gave a sudden shiver as though she had been struck with a draught. "We put a metal lid on.

"That won't keep *him* out," Esther replied.

The rain beat down, darkening the street, drumming on the roof. Water twisted from the gutters in a steady stream. Normally, she liked the rain but today it made the bakery too small, too hot. She opened her slicker but felt no relief.

"What are you going to do?" Helga asked. She was running loaves of bread through the slicer, then enclosing them in plastic bags.

"Nothing," Esther said, her voice echoing foolishly about her head. She could see Dominic sitting behind his desk, his hat still on. Unable to see his face, she imagined it yellow as a dying leaf.

"You can't do that." Helga gave the blue tin tie a twist. "They won't let you sell milk and then what'll you do? You

31

don't sell milk, you can't feed the cows. You can't feed the cows, you've got to sell them. You sell the cows, then what? If you don't let him have the trees, he'll get everything—barn, house, land. Mark my word. You'll be able to put all your belongings into a suitcase."

Her logic was remorseless. Esther knew the pattern by heart. She had seen other dairy farmers go under.

Only Dominic's arm moved. His large, shapeless hat was bent over the desk. Figuring, she thought. Figuring the profits on her trees. All the arrangements would already have been made. He knew who would cut them, who would haul them, who would turn them to veneer. She imagined him sitting in the car, the window rolled down while his son skipped about the trees with a tape.

"How big is that?"

"Six feet around, Pa."

"Is that branch rotten or solid?"

He would miss nothing and everything he saw would go down in crabbed jerky letters in the black notebook he always kept with him.

"I have to go," Esther said and, to excuse her sudden desire to leave, lied. "I just remembered. I left my kitchen window open."

Out in the truck, she sat, unable to make a decision about where to go. She wished she had someone to visit but the local people were not much for visiting. Like herself, they were usually too busy to waste time in idleness. Weddings and funerals were important enough to disrupt their routines. Those and fires.

From habit, she turned along the road toward her farm. The surface of the road was slippery and since she was indecisive about where she wanted to go, she drove slowly. Rain foamed from the windows until the thin, black wipers could not keep the glass clear. She stopped the truck, turned

32

off the motor and waited, her mind as empty as a polished glass bowl. For five minutes the rain beat on the truck, filling it with the roar of a thousand hammers on tin. She wished that it would go on forever. Suddenly, it eased so that she could see the road again. In the ditches, water was streaming away toward the creek.

She turned the key. The starter whined but the motor did not turn over. She tried twice more, then the cab filled with the smell of gasoline and she knew she had flooded the engine. Leaving the truck, she began to walk. The clay stuck to her boots so that, in a minute, her feet had grown grotesquely as though she had some terrible, debilitating disease. She tried to kick off the mud, then gave it up when one boot flew off and she had to hop after it.

"It always acts up in the rain," her hired man said. "Just like my kidneys."

He was hanging onto the doorframe, leaning out toward her, his blotched face resigned to disaster, his breath reeking of liquor. His left eye twitched constantly as though somewhere in his head a circuit was malfunctioning.

Her legs, because of the mud on her boots, were so tired that she could barely lift them. "I want you to take the tractor and get it."

"No need." He tipped his head back and let the rain fall into his upturned face. "Rain'll stop in five minutes. Wiring'll be dry in an hour. Then I can drive it back."

She knew there was no use trying to force him to go right away. He would only have an attack of pain and take to his bed.

"Dominic wants to cut down the walnut trees."

"Saw his car," he admitted. Quickly, proving he had already been thinking about it, he added, "You'll need to hire somebody to take out the stumps. I'm beyond it."

She had been going to say to him that she would not sell

the trees and his assumption that she had already let Dominic have them left her feeling defeated. If she had not been afraid of his contempt, she would have sat down in the mud and cried.

"We've got to get new wiring for the truck," he said. "The insulation's rotted. If you had some money, we could get it done."

Realizing that he was waiting for her to leave, she swung one heavy foot around and went to the house. As she scraped her boots with a piece of shingle, she studied the trees.

The sky dripped. The open spaces between the rows of milo narrowed, growing so small that it seemed no-one could force his way through the distant wall of brown, sword-like leaves, leaves so brown and stiff that the rain could darken but not soften them. Beyond them, the walnut trees, freshened by rain, floated, a soft island of green. It might have been an oasis, resting above miles of desolate sand.

There were 53 trees and the largest ones were so large that she could not reach around them. In spite of all that needed to be done, she had always seen to it that the trees were sprayed for bag worms and pruned. At night, she slept with the window open and, often, when she woke for no discernible reason, she leaned to the window, listening for the sound of a saw. Log rustlers abounded. They drifted through the Missouri nights, cutting down trees with muffled chain saws.

Once she had wakened to hooded lights, the soft drift of men's lowered voices, the dull roar of a saw. She had not hesitated. Taking down her father's rifle, she had crept to the yard, balanced the rifle on the edge of the manure wagon and started firing. She had emptied the rifle, loaded it and kept shooting. Her hired man had come running in a panic so total that he never remembered to put on boots. When she finished using the second magazine, they were standing like a spectacle in the middle of the yard, her in her night-gown and him in a suit of long underwear. In the darkness, he might have been a headless, handless, footless ghost. She refused to wait until morning and insisted they check on the trees immediately. She went first, between two rows of milo, rifle in hand. Protesting, her hired man slopped along behind, carrying a flashlight.

"They're just trees," he had cried. "Why've you got to look at them now?" When he had gone back for the flash-light, he had pulled on rubber boots, an ankle-length coat and jammed on his hat. Moonilght, he firmly believed, shin-ing on a bare head, drove men mad.

"They rest my eyes," she had replied and had kept him at her side until they had inspected every tree.

One of the trunks had a foot-long slash in it but it was not so deep as to be fatal so she had gone back to bed. In the morning, she had taken a propane stove, a pot and a large chunk of tar out to the grove and tarred the cut. Since that night no-one had fooled around with her trees.

The rain was stopping. She looked at her watch and saw that it was noon hour so she went inside to cook beans and make coffee.

Late that afternoon, her uncle appeared, riding high on his tractor. He had come to borrow her harrow.

"I heard you're getting your trees cut."

"Dominic made me an offer," she replied noncommitally. Evereyone, it seemed, knew her business.

"$50 a tree. I'd ask for $100. He'll pay it." He grunted as he tried to bend over to pick up a wrench. He was nearly as round and stiff-bodied as his hogs. "You got to put in new equipment."

"I'd rather not cut them."

"You can plant more."

"I guess," she said.

He was having a hard time loosening a nut and his hand slipped so that he scraped his knuckles. "Hot damn!" he exclaimed. He sucked at his knuckles and spit. He was a man without imagination or manners. He ploughed through life head down, his shoulders thrust forward and his eyes shut to everything except what was directly ahead of him. "It'll mean more grazing. Every little bit of grass helps. It's not as though the trees were good for anything. The nuts you get from them aren't worth more than a few dollars."

"That isn't the point," she said but he gave no indication that he had heard her.

After he had driven away, she walked back to the front porch and leaned against the corner post. The sky had cleared but the light had been drawn from it so that it was as pale as ice skimmed from the top of a bucket. The milo was darker than before, the leaves heavier, as though they had taken on a great weight and were pressing into the earth.

She feasted her eyes on the trees. Shot through with light, polished by rain, the leaves were as clear as glass.

Along the fence, the Holsteins were approaching. They followed one another in a long procession, unhurried and dignified. The bell of the lead cow, its clapper beating against the square sides of metal, was dull and flat, without rhythm or beauty, but it was too insistent to be ignored. There was no use her going to begin anything else so Esther waited. In a little while, the lead cow would reach the gate and then Esther would have to walk across the yard, let down the bar and stand aside, waiting until the cows had all passed through the gap. Then she would put the bar back in place and follow them into the barn to see that they were milked and fed.

It happened that way every night.

Travelling On

Beth Harvor

Their furniture left Toronto three hours before they did; so it had travelled along the same highway and toward the same destination. When they got on the bus Natasha had suggested the children sit together and so they sat on the seat behind her, sharing a pile of comic books and a polythene bag of oranges and apples. Her seat-mate as far as Peterborough was a black-haired boy with round eyes and tanned pock-marked skin, a student at Trent. By the time they were half an hour out of Toronto she knew that he had broken off with his fiancée (she was spoiled rotten); that his dream was to go to a fair-sized city, like Ottawa, open a discotheque, make a lot of money; that he never read fiction. He liked to have things settled, he only read technical books.

What had brought on this last confession, or boast, was the pile of books in her lap—Munro's *Lives of Girls and Women*, an astrology book, de Beauvoir's *The Woman Destroyed*, a collection of fairy-tales she'd found wedged in under one of the sun-porch windows just before they'd left the house.

She asked him if he'd had fairy-tales read to him when he was little.

He couldn't recall that he had.

"Did you read a lot in your family?" he asked her.

"When I was a child, you mean? Yes, we did. We read to each other. Especially in the winter. We lived on an island out in the Atlantic." This last statement always sounded so poetic, so outlandish—like her name, (and the island had been responsible for her name too—*War and Peace* had been the perfect bedside companion for a long winter pregnancy), that whenever she made it, she was always surprised that people believed it. She usually found herself driven to modify it, to mention that the island was close to the mainland, close to the coast of Maine, and that it was acually situated in the Bay of Fundy and not out on the open sea. But she saw that with him this would not be necessary. Nothing in his cool round eyes suggested she should feel obliged to either account for or diminish her romantic past. He was simply sitting there, waiting for her to continue. She continued: "My mother liked to be read to. While she worked. While she was dropping off to sleep. While she was taking her bath. *The Adventures of Sherlock Holmes.* Travel books. Dickens. For her, I think, reading was like sex. Someone could do it to you, but you must never do it to yourself."

A smile flickered between his cheeks. It went well with his round eyes, the blues of his T-shirt and jeans. He stretched. "Man," he said, "I must remember that the next time I take a book to bed with me."

Natasha smiled; she saw herself at nine or ten. 1945. 1946. Two wings of dark hair leading into the tributaries of two tiny thin black baby braids which fed, in turn, into two long fat shiny black ropes of hair. She heard her mother calling out to her (from her bath, from her bed) "Tash darling, come and read to me!" She remembered how she had felt: both honoured and interfered with. And, of course, as she had got older, less and less honoured, more and more interfered with. Still it had taken her some time to discover how intensely her mother desired attention. Even when her mother had been, technically speaking, "audience," she had renounced the role; in her bath and as she slept, always and everywhere, she had been centre-stage. So it must have been only the act that mattered. *Being read to.* The words had apparently been mere background music to the performance of her mother "listening." Natasha was sure she hadn't heard more than a key phrase or two a page, the words seemed to have washed over her, like ocean water, and with that kind of attention-span her tastes had naturally been catholic—Gogol, A. J. Cronin, it was all the same to her. . . .

"How's the discotheque situation in Ottawa?" the student was asking her. She told him that she didn't know, that she had only visited Ottawa twice, that the first time (during her honeymoon, in the late fifties) it had seemed an ugly city—filled with grim stone government castles, potholes, slush and dun-coloured wooden barracks-like office buildings built during the Second World War, still standing now, as far as she knew, and still called temporary. . . .

("Lady," he said, "You must have had one lousy honeymoon." She spread out her naked hands.

"Separated," she said. He nodded.) Then later, in the late sixties, her husband and her two children, Adam and Frances, who were sitting just behind them now, had gone there on holiday and the city had been transformed into a discreet carnival city of swans, pedestrian malls, red-and-white awnings, outdoor restaurants, boat trips along the canal. She told him that they were moving to Ottawa now, that her ex-husband or her estranged husband or whatever he was had found a house for them there, that it would be good for the children to be closer to their father, that they needed a father, that her friends in Toronto had advised against the move, that *they* thought it meant that she wanted to get together with her husband again, but that that wasn't true.

"I know what you mean," he said. "I still run into my old girlfriend sometimes. A beautiful girl. Beautiful. And do you know what? Every time I see her I congratulate myself. I congratulate myself that I'm no longer tied up to that beautiful girl." He shook his head in wonder. "People on the outside," he said, "Friends, acquaintances, what do they know? Nothing! The anger, it stays fresh. . ." The bus pulled into the Peterborough depot. He gracefully reached up and fetched his bag. "Well goodbye," he said, and then, with a mock-leer, "Enjoy your reading." They both smiled. "And good luck," he said.

"Good luck to you too," she said. He was off, ducking down through the doorway.

The eyes and hands of Frances and Adam appeared over the edge of the leather seats; they looked like two little birds peering over the rims of two nests.

"Who was that man, Mummy? What were you talking about?"

"A college boy," she said. "We were talking about Ottawa and books and things like that. How's the food holding out?"

She twisted around to look. In the polythene bag, the single remaining apple and the single remaining orange were lying in a brown sauce, a cold fog, were lying in the wet and debris of their own cores and skins.

"I think I'll come up and sit with you," Adam said. But just then an old woman came along the aisle and sat down beside Natasha; and she found that for the moment she preferred this old stranger to her own known young son. If the old woman talked, she could open one of her books and read. If Adam talked, she would have to talk back. She raised her eyes in a gesture of helplessness to Adam. He looked lost. Frances looked pleased. (It wouldn't have been fair to Frances, either, she thought, but it was a thought that was hypocritical because it came too late.)

"Frances," she said then, reminding herself most terribly of her own mother, "Why don't you read aloud to Adam?"

"Oh Mummy!" Frances cried, "I don't want to!"

And they both went back to their comics.

"Are those your children?" the old woman asked her.

"Yes," she said, thinking *I could have been sitting with Adam!* She opened the book on astrology that she had bought at the bus terminal. (The old woman was too old to care about astrology, too old even to have been interested in it in the thirties; with someone young, taking out a book on astrology would have been dangerous, but with the old woman she was safe). And Natasha began, severely, to read. She was a moon child. It sounded better than Cancer. John was Aquarius. According to the book, Aquarius was not a very good mate for Cancer. Good, she was glad to see that. All I want to know, she thought, is will I live or die? And will I find love? And happiness. And will I find a job? She turned to the section that began:

MOON CHILD: YOUR PERSONALIZED FORECAST FOR THE FUTURE

Uranus is having a strong influence on Cancerians now— and will do so for several years, until 1977. This indicates changes in both work and residential environments. You may have to change living habits and habitats, move considerable distances.

HUMAN RELATIONSHIPS

You've but recently gotten clear of some confining influences in this area, and there are several years of increased and expanded social activity and a number of fine new friendships ahead.

41

There will be major changes in the marriage situations of Cancerians who are already married. Uranus will have a powerful influence and could cause dissension, estrangement, separation, divorce.

My God, she thought, this is fantastic. She looked up the section on THE CANCERIAN PERSONALITY (for the June 22nd–July 23rd synchronicity-span) and learned that she was sensitive, imaginative, emotional and tenacious. She looked up her moon sign and was advised to read the delineations for both Virgo and Libra since the moon had moved from Virgo to Libra some time during the day of her birth and she didn't know her birth time. Because of this, there was no way she could tell what her rising sign was either. She read the influence Libra and Virgo moon would have on Cancer sun. She looked up the moon signs of John, of Adam, of Frances, of her mother. Then the bus pulled into the stop-over place and they all got stiffly out. The stop-over place was a kind of chalet, set in rolling farm country. They walked across a cold sunny concrete plaza that was walled by weeds. The lodge was large and clean and, at that time of day, in late afternoon sun, very bright. There were little maxims on paper made to look like birch bark in frames of miniature brown plastic logs. Natasha shivered. "Come," she said to Frances, "Let's go into the Ladies' Room." They worked their way in. Their was a crowd in front of the sinks and mirrors, outlining their lips, outlining their eyes, repairing the damage from so many hours of sitting still. Natasha looked at herself in the full-length mirror—at her puckish tanned face, her short black hair, black pants, white t-shirt, big breasts. ("Cancer women have beautiful breasts.") She moved cautiously toward her own image like someone approaching a fine but unpredictable animal. She took out her eye-shadow and did up her eyes, to give herself a reason for being there, stationed at her own reflection. "Do your business, Franny," she said, "Then we'll go get something to eat." Three toilets flushed in rapid succession, Natasha disposed of the polythene bag of garbage, Frances came out of her cubicle, they went together and stood in line to get at one of the sinks. They washed their hands, then they went out into the cafeteria and found Adam. They got into another line and each got a plate of spaghetti and a little hospital-style plastic glass of apple juice. The bus driver was sitting in a special part of the cafeteria separated from the main part by a heavy red rope. The children looked at him dully as they ate. They were very tired. Everything is going to be all right, Natasha thought, "The changes have all been for the best, you'll realize, as overlapping benign influences build into an eleven-year cycle of complete environmental harmony for you beginning in summer, 1977." They went outside and climbed into the bus and although there were now many empty seats, they went to their own seats as if they had been programmed to sit in them, and them only. The old lady came and sat down beside Natasha again too. This time she didn't speak, and Natasha looked out the window. For a while she looked at the banks of alders and the pelts of rich grass that ran along the highway, and at the high flanks of grass where the road had been cut between hills, and then at the trees that had been killed by the water they stood in—the murderous element now covered by green scum, and except for flat stretches of open farming country, the whole trip was like that, endlessly repeating over and over: pelts, flanks, swamps—all green. Later in the afternoon she started watching the clouds; there was a giant illuminated cauliflower (Victorian gilt behind Hiroshima-image) and there was also the Duke of Windsor lying in bed. His cloud-cover got fleecy down by what, given

43

a more robust royal legend, might have been called his sex. Then night came on and the sky cleared completely and there was only the evening star in it, and one other star, a far low red one, that could have been a plane or a radio tower. And then she could look out her window and see the small rectangular moon that was someone's reading-light travelling along beside them. Farther away was another moon that moved along fast with the bus. This moon was moon-sized and moon-shaped but it had the ability to go through trees and houses as if they were invisible, as if they were water, and sometimes it did an opposite trick, mid-sky, and disappeared entirely. Fugitive moon for fugitive lady. The truth was, it fit. She had wanted to escape Toronto at least as much as she had wanted to bring the children to their father's city. The reason was she had fallen in love in Toronto. Fallen in love, as one is fallen in battle. A younger man, maybe even as much as fifteen years younger. Even in bed she'd never asked him his age. She had had the worldly woman's discretion—based simply and practically on terror of the truth. He had rented a room from her when he'd first come to the city (he was an American, the friend of a friend, come to Canada to teach courses on film at Sheridan and York) and he'd been astounded by Canadian prices for food and rent. So he'd asked his friends if they knew of a place he could stay while he took his time to find a decent apartment. Natasha was recommended. At first she had not been particularly attracted to him although she had certainly, and immediately, liked him. He had long frizzy fair hair tied back with a dull black ribbon and he wore army pants and an alligator belt. But his shirts were man-of-the-world shirts—mauve, pink, even a pinstripe one with cufflinks. There was a little rosy moon of bald spot under the fine fair hair (sadly premature) and he had brown eyes that shone with sweet judgment and hands so sinewy that in his

44

younger youth he might have played the piano. Or killed someone. And he probably had: she did not believe the army pants were an affectation. (But they never talked about the war.) His name was Jacob Barlow and she guessed he was about 24. Her ability to gauge his age left her soon after that, a measure of how quickly she'd fallen under his spell, although there were a few deceptively level-headed days of secretly comparing herself and Jacob with Colette and Maurice Goudeket, and even with Agatha Christie and Sir Max. But in the end she'd lacked Colette's and Christie's energy and faith. The faith first, the energy later. And Jacob. For that and possibly other less flattering reasons he weaned her. Less bed, more conversation. Then less conversation. Finally less everything. In spite of the outrageous rents, he found himself an apartment. In four weeks it was all over; his books and his bags and his own shining presence and smile and his young but fatherly way of paying attention to her were all gone. She thought she would die. She spent hours of every day reproaching herself. That she had been too honest with him, that she had not been honest enough, that she had, in spite of her greater age, been too innocent, that she'd been too serious with him or too silly. Toronto became a sad city, there were a dozen streets where whole conversations would return to her, streets where they'd walked apartment-hunting, or only pretending to apartment-hunt (in the hopeful beginning), and the breakfast table became sad too, with remembered talk, and the way he'd looked at her certain times—turning once, by the kitchen stove, to look at her a certain way because of something she'd said, if she didn't stop remembering that and everything else, the pain of it all might destroy her. And after he left she went through a period—mercifully short— of writing hopeful letters to him, (the silliest, emptiest, and certainly longest letters she'd ever written to anyone) and when he didn't reply she felt compassion for him and even approval. No anger. He was right after all. She would not have been up to it in the end. The sooner it was all stopped the better. And an image of herself growing older started to haunt her—being forced to add every kind of fortitude to her dry-powder arsenal. And so she gave up. But she was not cured. And the following spring, when her husband, who for over a year had been wanting the children closer to him, found a possible place for them to live in Ottawa, not far from his own apartment, she decided it made sense after all to go and live there.

In Ottawa, Natasha's allergy serum had been standing in the refrigerator for over two weeks, wedged in between the butter and the eggs. And the lives of the people who ate the butter and the eggs were beginning to take shape, to settle—they had each learned the names of some of the people on their block, and sometimes John came over with some special pastries for the children (from the Rideau Bakery), and a bag of dirty laundry for Natasha. The astrology book said: "You may have the urge to play the victim or be a martyr. Do not satisfy this urge." She did up his laundry anyway, and fed him too, if he arrived at mealtime; after all, he was paying the rent. But he had not changed. Ottawa, on the other hand, had. It was neither the city of the honeymoon nor the city of the holiday. Or maybe it hadn't changed at all, maybe the real city, the city that lay beyond the official buildings and driveways and parks, was emerging at last. Natasha spent the early days there consultings maps and lists, learning the bus routes, finding grocery stores, finding a place where she could get copies of the key made for the children, finding a place where she could get heels put on Adam's shoes. The foreign language that she heard spoken all around her was not Italian, as in Toronto, but a nasal, congested Ottawa Valley French. As she made her rounds, hearing the French, smelling the grass, she made definite statements to herself. This city has a lot of trees. This city has a lot of water. It was a way of getting her bearings. As for the spring, it was far advanced in Ottawa, and since the city was dotted with parks and surrounded by a greenbelt and sitting in a valley, a valley that had the Gatineau Hills greenly pollinating to the north, it was a bad place for sufferers from hayfever. Toronto, on the other hand, had been good this spring. It hadn't had her husband in it. And it had been on a great lake. The second Sunday she was in Ottawa, Natasha got very sick. Flu, sinus infection and allergy hit her all at once—she was groggy and feverish, she had chills, she felt she could hardly breathe. (The astrology book said: "There is no-one able to come down with a migraine headache, a severe sinus or asthma attack more quickly or convincingly than a moon child.") She decided that one of the first things she had to do when she got better was find a doctor who could give her her allergy shots once a week, a man who could double as a doctor for her children. She got the name of a Dr. Robert H. Dudiak from one of her neighbours and one afternoon in early June, while her children were at school, she went to his office.

As she pushed open the door of Dr. Dudiak's office, Natasha saw that the room was half-filled with people. She picked out a chair near the magazine table. The nurse appeared at the receptionist's window.

"You have an appointment?"

"Yes. I'm Mrs. Morissey."

"First name?" the nurse asked her, beginning to type. She was a small, trim woman with black hair parted in the middle and pulled into a tiny bun at the back of the neck.

47

She had a surprisingly loud voice.

"Natasha."

"*Natasha*. That's a new one. You'll have to spell it."

Natasha spelled it.

"And your OHIP number?"

She produced it.

"All right, Natasha Morissey," the nurse said, "I've got your number. And *my* name, by the way, is Mrs. Savage. Mrs. Mary Savage." She indicated a little black plastic stand that acted as a support for the white plastic letters: MRS. MARY SAVAGE, R. N. "Otherwise known as the happy cannibal," the nurse said.

A few people smiled. "Mary Savage. Happy cannibal," the nurse said.

And Natasha made two statements to herself. *This nurse likes an audience. This nurse reminds me of my mother.* And nothing that happened that afternoon made her revise this first impression. "Hello there, Linda Wilson!" the nurse would cry in her big voice, "How's that baby of yours?" or "Hi, big boy, how's Bobby Charbonneau?" One way and another she imposed herself on the group of captive people in the room—addressing them by both first and last names, answering one phone and then putting it on hold while she was answering the other, putting *that* on hold while she went back to the first, breaking into that conversaion to call out something to the doctor, breaking ino her own conversaion with the doctor to ask someone to come in and get her blood checked, talking as she typed, breaking into her typing to take the blood, breaking into the taking of the blood to go back to the phone, asking the person on the phone to wait while she typed the blood, carrying the whole show on, as much as was possible, in front of the receptionist's window. Even when she was off-stage briefly, in the treatment room, say, they could still hear her voice, bullying, making

48

jokes, keeping them all up to date on the astonishing range of her enterprises. And yet at the moment when Natasha's disapproval of the nurse reached a very high intensity, the nurse engaged in something that could only be called compassionate interference and Natasha thought: Maybe she isn't such a monster after all. What had happened was this: a girl had come in. A girl with her arm in a sling. This girl was in her early twenties, fat but pretty. But there was something wrong about her; she had a grotesque collection of long coarse black whiskers growing from the soft white underpart of her chin. People didn't want to stare, you could see that immediately. Their eyes dropped—to their magazines, to their laps. Natasha tried to read a magazine. She could feel the girl sitting right beside her, to her left. She did not look up. Then the nurse popped up, like one half of a Punch-and-Judy show. Oh God, thought Natasha, spare us your wisecracks, Nurse.

"Hello, Lorna Maranda!" the nurse shouted, "People will think you've got a growth of whiskers there! Is it today you get the stitches out?" And it was as if the nurse had broken a spell. They all looked up at the girl. "I hope so," said Lorna Maranda. "I guess I should have got them to put them in with white thread." She had a slight English accent. "Then it would have looked like an old woman's stubble," said Natasha, remembering suddenly the old woman who had sat beside her on the bus. The girl sighed and smiled. "Right," she said. "I guess I should have got them to put them in with purple thread."

"Were you in a car accident?" Natasha asked her.

"Yeah. On Sunday. It was raining, remember? We went over to take a look at the ditch." She sighed the blissful, philosophical sigh of the survivor. "We got a little too close," she said.

"Were you driving?"

"No. I was in the death seat." She smiled again. "My sister was driving. My sister had a gash on her forehead and she was covered with blood. Mud and blood. Six cars stopped to help us. The first people were in a station wagon and it was the first day of their vacation. The husband went off to call an ambulance and the wife climbed down into the ditch with a brand new beach towel and she used that to make a sling for my arm. People were very kind. My sister got hysterical. She was jumping around in the mud like she'd lost something. When the ambulance came it took us to a beautiful little hospital in a small town out in the country. When the doctor there saw us he started singing, *Mud, Mud, Glorious Mud*. And the nurse there made a point, *actually made a point*, of cutting my dress down the seam when they had to cut my clothes off me. You wouldn't get that kind of consideration in any of the hospitals *here*—not at the Civic or the General, they'd just tear the clothes off you, anything for speed and efficiency. . . actually they took us to the General when they got us back into town. If you're ever in an accident, don't go to the General," she advised the room at large. "When I had to phone my boss about it I said, "You're not going to believe this. . ." I've been sick so much lately. Last month I sprained my ankle and this month I was off two weeks with the flu. . ."

"Maybe it's not a good time for you," said Natasha.

"That could be," said the girl.

"Maybe there was something wrong with your stars. Maybe the aspects were bad. . ."

"I'm a moon child," said Lorna Maranda.

"So am I," said Natasha. "And I was feeling very sick on Sunday too. I had the flu. Actually, 1973 isn't supposed to be a very good year for people born under Cancer. Although it gets better as it goes on. I just bought a book on astrology and it says that things get better and better from 1974

50

on. . ." Oh God, she thought, I sound like an idiot. "If you believe that sort of thing," she said.

But Lorna Maranda was not self-conscious.

"That's good," she said, "I could stand for things to get better, let me tell you." And she started to tell Natasha about how she would be moving to Toronto next year and changing her job.

The nurse had been in and out answering the phone and typing but she must have been quieter than usual. Natasha noticed her once again when three new people came in. A boy and two girls. The boy had the kind of colouring that in an older more self-confident man might have been described as florid, but which in the boy had condensed itself into the flush of someone who hates to be on display. The two girls looked tanned and self-contained. They both had straight fair hair and pale shift dresses. Natasha thought they must be sisters. The older one was about eighteen; the younger nine or ten.

"Well, Chris Podoski!" the nurse cried, "I see you've brought your harem with you."

The flush deepened. "I left the rest of them outside."

"You didn't have an appointment, did you, Leslie Van Velthoven?" the nurse asked the taller girl. Her voice was not as friendly when she talked to the girl as it had been when she'd talked to the boy.

The girl shook her head.

"And who's the young lady?" the nurse asked the girl.

"This is my sister Saskia," said the girl. "We just came along to keep Chris company."

"Have you finished school, Leslie?" the nurse asked the girl.

The girl said yes.

"I see you've been getting some sun."

The girl smiled.

The nurse started dialling a number and then, in the middle of dialling, suddenly put down the phone. She left the receptionist's chair and opened the door to the waiting room and stood there on the threshold in full view of everyone.

"Leslie," she said in a firm clear voice, "Didn't I read something about your brother in the paper? Didn't I read that he had died?"

"Yes," said Leslie, "On Sunday, in Holland. In Amsterdam."

"Was it an accident?"

"Yes," said Leslie.

"And haven't your parents been away?"

"Yes they were," said Leslie, "But they've come back home now."

(Sunday, Sunday, Natasha was thinking: What was his sign? "You are not simple shallow people," the book had said. "You would never deliberately hurt anyone. With Saturn on your sun and Neptune in your house of health you may feel tired at times, even exhausted. Be extremely careful of food and water in foreign habitats. . ." Food poisoning, thought Natasha, or maybe he drowned. . .) And the nurse seemed to have run out of questions.

"Well I'm very sorry to hear that, Leslie," was what she finally said. And she went back into the recptionist's room.

Except for one quick frightened look at Leslie (who seemed to be holding herself together all right) Natasha found she couldn't look at anyone any more. A kind of pall had fallen over the waiting room. They were all in their own worlds, as they had been at the beginning—a frozen galaxy. And within the frame of the receptionist's window, the nurse began again to shine, typing a little, calling out to the doctor a little, talking on two phones at once a little, ordering EKGs and blood tests a little, and calling all the patients by their first and last names together.

When the happy cannibal called her in for her shot, Natasha was carrying one of the doctor's magazines with her, opened at an article on women writers. Mrs. Savage didn't make any comment on it but the doctor, when he came in, drying his hands on a white towel, said "What's that you're reading?" and so she showed him.

He snorted. He was a young man still, with a sensual ape-like face, little round steel-rimmed glasses, teasing eyes. He said that there were no women writers, no great ones. No great women artists at all. No great women poets, no great women composers. Name me one, he said. Name me just one great woman artist. He was smiling.

She named him eight or nine of them, beginning with Flannery O'Connor and ending with Isak Dinesen.

"I've never heard of the last one. Or the first one either, for that matter. Some relative of Frank O'Connor's is she? A cousin maybe?"

"She's an American. Dead now. Very great. She's been compared to Sophocles."

"Sophocles," he said, smiling at her again. "Now I do believe I have heard of him."

"And Isak Dinesen felt obliged to write under a man's name, so you see what men have done to women. Her real name was Karen Blixen. And you should hear this: when Ernest Hemingway was given the Nobel prize for literature he said it should have gone to Isak Dinesen."

"Never one of my favourites, Hemingway," said Dr. Dudiak.

Mrs. Savage asked her if she had read a book called *Total*

53

Woman.

She said no.

"Women should stay as sweet as they are," said Mrs. Savage. "That's what this book says."

The next time she went for her shot the waiting room was empty. The radio in the nurse's room was on though, playing dance music from the fifties, and there was a bottle of Coke with a pink-and-white striped straw in it standing on the nurse's desk.

Mrs. Savage came out from one of the treatment rooms. She said that Dr. Dudiak had been held up at the hospital— a baby—and that all the other appointments had been cancelled.

"I tried to reach you too," she said, "but there was no answer."

"I was downtown," said Natasha. "I stopped in here on my way home."

And then a call came from the doctor saying he was on his way back, so she decided to wait. The nurse started to tell her things about her private life, that she was a widow, that her husband had dropped dead from a heart attack two years before, that she missed him so much, still. She said that one day about a year after he died, she'd come home from working at Dr. Dudiak's, when all of a sudden going into the empty apartment had frightened her. She hadn't been scared of theives or anything like that—it was just a feeling about the place. She had stepped just far enough into the apartment to throw her cap and cape onto the bed and to reach her car-coat out of the closet. Then she'd gone down to the basement garage and got into her car and got right clear out of the city, quick as was legal. She had driven all night that night, with no company but the radio and through more dark woods than she'd ever known existed, stopping only for gas and chocolate bars. Natasha was affected by the story of this journey; her feeling toward the nurse was altered by it. Her knowledge of Mrs. Savage was now piece-meal but deep—as if the woman had stepped out on a stage before her with a monologue which, though short, made a definite but puzzling contribution to the larger text of a play.

After that she didn't go back to the doctor's for a long time. Summer came, the allergy lifted, Dr. Dudiak went away on vacation. In August she hit on the idea of setting up a course on women writers, a hybrid thing, something between consciousness-raising and instruction, for a community college on the outskirts of the city. She had several meetings with a man in the Department of Continuing Education out there, a tired-eyed man who didn't quibble about credentials. She told him that she didn't have any, no academic ones, but that she had read a great deal, referred from the jacket of one women's book to another, moving from Lessing to Mortimer, from Mortimer to O'Brien, from O'Brien to Colette, from Colette to Canadian women; except for Colette, these names were not familiar to him but, as he said, "We like self-starters here. This is what community education is supposed to be all about." And so she was hired.

Two weeks before the course was due to begin she panicked and phoned a friend of a Toronto friend, described the course to her, was invited to a coffee party that morning in Rockcliffe.

She decided to walk up there. It turned out to be a long walk, though pleasant, deep into Rockcliffe Village, past every kind of architectural jewel and aberration. Her visual sense was heightened, by nervousness and hope, to that of an observant tourist; she still did not feel at home in this city. She took note of stone urns with geraniums in them, women coming out of houses in tennis dresses, the green of the grass turned to sparkle by sprinklers. The house of the friend of the Toronto friend turned out to be grand too, but it had a kind of Georgian restraint, offset by women and small children—all brown-skinned and in brief, bright bird-of-paradise clothes. Her hostess, a girl called Gerry— barefoot, baby-blue jeans, bird-of-paradise blouse—took Natasha under her wing and introduced her to the most hopeful prospects; that morning alone she signed up ten definites and two possibles and by the time the course day rolled around the community college told her there would be eighteen women in her group.

That day was a bad day, distinguished by cold-sweat terror and regret. What had possessed her? How could she have ever imagined she was qualified to do anything like this? How arrogant, what foolhardy arrogance, to imagine that she could step out of a domestic life and into the role of teacher and group leader! She, who had never taught, who'd had no training in it, who was ordinarily so shy that even making her voice carry at gatherings of more than five or six people caused a pain like a burning cramp the whole length of her throat. Where had this arrogance come from? From living on an island? Big frog in little pond? (The island certainly qualified as a little pond.) From reading aloud to her mother? She had come to read aloud so well, in fact, that when she'd got older she'd finally seen the error of her ways, had finally seen that she'd come to sound like an elocutionist, and so she'd deliberately overhauled her voice, dismantled and humanized it, introduced a hitch there, a flaw here, made it more gravelly and amusing. But the voice was the least of her worries—unless her still-ridiculous faith in it spurred her to use it for reading when she should be talking or to use it for talking when she should be listening. And this brought her to the real problem: how was she to choose how she wanted to be—mother or dazzler? Which ability should she hone—provided she was even in possession of either—the ability to hold people's attention or the sense to know when to shut up and let other people have the limelight? Should she reflect or should she shine. She knew that the answer to that was both, but she also felt she couldn't lie to herself here; leaders had styles and in deciding whether her style was to be elitist or egalitarian she would be deciding what she wanted most: not just in tonight's class but for all the time: respect or love. With a terrible cold-sweat sinking of the heart she knew it was love.

Trembling, sweating, sick to her stomach with fear, she started putting on water for tea, filled up a saucepan from the tap, put it on the stove. But five minutes later, when she was loading her supply of women's books ino a cardboard carton, she suddenly remembered she'd forgotten to put the heat on under the saucepan. On her way to the stove she remembered she wanted to make herself some toast and she sliced a piece of bread, but instead of putting it in the toaster or remembering to turn on the stove she carried the un-buttered bread over to the table with her and with her free hand took out and opened two books she'd marked off to read aloud from for the first evening's class—the first was *Memoirs of a Dutiful Daughter* (de Beauvoir learning to read); the second was *Earthly Paradise* (Colette being reprimanded for preferring, in a school essay, the beauties of fall to spring).

She was deep in *Earthly Paradise*, her bread half-eaten, when a condensed terrible wail filled the air at the side of the house. She dropped the book on the table and ran to the kitchen door and opened it. There was Adam, running up the stairs toward her, cupping a bloody hand in a good one, (for a hopeful second she'd thought it was a hurt bird he

57

was holding), with a retinue of shouting explaining children coming up the stairs behind him. The cut was so deep looking down into it made her dizzy. But at the edge of her dizziness, which she knew even then was her indecision, something yellow was easing itself in behind the leaves of next door's driveway. So she pushed past all the explaining children and ran down the steps with Adam in tow, crying out to her neighbour: "My child's got a bad cut, can you drive us to the doctor's?"

When they came into Dr. Dudiak's waiting room Natasha's left hand was bloody from holding Adam's hand together in the car; the right hand still held the piece of bread she'd been eating when he'd come screaming to the door. There was a differrnt nurse at the desk this time—a pale fair-haired girl whispering into the phone—and when she saw Adam's hand (not the cut, but only the red spittle and drool escaping his fist) she took them into the treatment room at once and went to get the doctor.

Adam had stopped crying and was now deathly pale. He was stretched out on the treatment table in his caked jeans and stinking sneakers and sweater with the holes in the elbows. He was holding his good hand clasped round his fist. With her free hand Natasha stroked his forehead.

Dr. Dudiak came in, looking at Adam's chart.

"Oh Adam," he said. "Let's see what you've been doing to yourself."

Adam dredged up a weak smile.

The doctor gently pried his hands apart.

"Where did this happen, Adam?"

"In the field across from my house."

"Glass, was it? Or was it a tin can?"

"A piece of glass."

"When did he last have a tetanus shot, do you remember?"

"Oh it was quite a long time ago. We were living in Toronto. I don't think we'd been living there very long. But I can't remember exactly when."

"We'd better give him that too then."

And Dr. Dudiak filled up a syringe with local anaesthetic, and started injecting it into the glistening sides of that little (but cavernous) gap of flesh. Adam yelped and turned to hide his face in the cleft in Natasha's thighs.

She held his head.

"It's going to be all right, Adam."

"It's okay for him to yell, it hurts like hell."

And so after that, except for Adam's little yelps, there was silence. Then Dr. Dudiak was finished and the hand was frozen and the tension melted.

Dr. Dudiak looked up at Natasha and smiled and said, "What's with you and the piece of bread?"

"I was just in the middle of eating it when he came to the door with his cut."

The doctor smiled.

"A lady who likes her lunch," she said.

"Just don't drop any crumbs in the wound," he said.

And he started to sew it up.

The treatment room now seemed like a nice place, with all the clinical rows of glass beakers and jars on all the glass shelves. Dr. Dudiak put six stitches in the cut. She could see he was good at sewing people up. While he was cutting off the thread-ends the new nurse walked by out in the hall. This made Natasha think of the old one.

"Where's the happy cannibal?"

Dr. Dudiak looked as if she had struck him.

"Are you referring to Mrs. Savage?"

The formality of this question struck her, even confused her; but didn't stop her.

"Yes. That's what she always calls herself, isn't it?"

"Mrs. Savage is dead," he said.

"*Dead?*" she whispered.

"She died three weeks ago."

It must have been an accident, she thought. She couldn't imagine that woman staying still long enough to incubate any disease.

"An accident?" she asked him, and she saw that Adam was turning toward him too, for his answer.

"Cancer," said Dr. Dudiak. "Liver." And she saw he was close to tears. He liked the happy cannibal, she thought. I suppose she was a good nurse, I suppose he misses her.

"By the time the pain came the disease was very advanced," said Dr. Dudiak. "Until two weeks before she died she seemed in perfect health."

Natasha recalled Mrs. Savage standing in the doorway to the waiting room, asking the girl about her dead brother. How amazing that Mrs. Savage should have been dying herself that day, unknown to herself and everyone else. And like a terrible vision she saw Mrs. Savage in the form of an advent calendar, a cut-out paper doll nurse in a uniform that was itself as crisp and pure as advent-calendar snow, with little doors all over her uniformed torso, to be opened on different dates, so that the plain white door over her liver would, when opened, reveal not a candle or an angel, but only a terrible picture of something diseased. We are all advent calendars, she thought, the pictures behind the doors are known only to the Calendar-Maker.

Of course the death of Mrs. Savage was a death out of context and so was naturally the more unbelievable because of it. If she had known the nurse was a secret drinker or came from a family prone to the disease she'd died from, her end would not have seemed so black magical and ordained.

"She seemed so energetic," she said.

But Dr. Dudiak really did look as if he might start to cry.

He turned from her and went over to the shelves by the sink to get the tetanus injection ready. She tried to think of something to keep him from crying, something they could argue about. She considered health foods, Vitamin E, acupuncture, but decided instead on their old stand-by. So she told him about the course she was going to be giving, starting that night, on women writers. It worked. He was immediately restored to normality, even enlivened; he snorted.

"You should take it," she said. "It would do you good."

He gave her a quick smile that was medical, tactical, grateful all at once. Then he gave Adam his shot. He put down the syringe, then touched Natasha lightly on the shoulder.

"Bring Adam back in seven days," he said, "to get his stitches out."

When Adam and Natasha came out from the doctor's there was a light fall wind blowing—carrying a city bouquet: the smells from a gas station, a bakery, a dry-cleaner's. Dusk bloomed in the vacant lot across the street, bloomed in the faded grass and brown bushes, free of the sick lavender pallor of the Queensway's mercury-vapour lights. They could walk home from here, along the village-like street that climbed the hill, and so they turned and walked into a fresher wind and in the hilly street's direction. Natasha discovered that her fear of the coming evening had left her completely (Adam's cut had saved her from that) and what she was thinking as they walked toward home was what did she have in the house for making a lightning-quick supper. There were two cans of Sockeye salmon in the cupboard. She could empty one of them out on their plates, along with a few dollops of mayonnaise and some sliced cucumbers and tomatoes. Frances could pour the milk and butter the bread. It shouldn't take more than three minutes, which would leave her with six or seven minutes to eat. They passed children who were playing and screaming in the street. Some of their faces were by now familiar to her and it was their faces that seemed to give a new and welcome feeling of familiarity to the whole street. Adam was aware of them too and walked by them with his good hand in his pocket and his bandaged one on display. A pity to rush him but if they proceeded at this wounded, measured pace they would never get there in time. Of course she could have phoned John from the doctor's to have him come to pick them up but she was glad, even elated, that she hadn't.

And it suddenly hit her that she would have an anecdote to begin the first night's class with; she could describe her conversations on women writers with Dr. Dudiak, who she could say an accident had again brought her into contact with only a few hours before. And at the thought of that, at the thought of Dr. Dudiak teasing her and telling her there were no women artists, she thought: men make it too easy for women; they drive us into contempt for them and out of our contempt into a sense of our own resourcefulness, they could make us mad with power in the end. But at that she could imagine the political women in the group crying out, *Power! We don't have power! Where have you been?* Safer to start with Adam's cut and how one fear had wiped out another. This could set off a discussion on women and their feelings in relation to children and work, or a discussion on women and fear. And at some point her experience with Jacob Barlow would come in useful. She was planning a session on the old woman, using Laurence's *The Stone Angel* and an article by de Beauvoir called *The Double Standard of Aging*. (But this would come later). Oh it was fine, really, it was all so fine, she felt such a sense of miraculous use in her own life and her own experience. She could consume her past, she could be nourished by defeats. Even Adam's name, although he had been christened with it because it was the name of a close friend of John's, seemed metaphorical for a moment—as if what they were rushing toward was more the revolution than their supper. This was the moment when she turned to him and said, "Adam, I'm sorry, but we'll have to hurry."

More Than Conquerors

Jack Hodgins

"Aw Gladdy, don't quit."

He could yell his lungs out, though, before she'd change her mind. Gladdy Roote lay there on that beach, gasping, and would have called herself an old half-dead seal foundered on rock if anyone asked.

She knew well enough that in a bathing suit she was a sight to see: flesh like slabs of goose-pimpled lard, legs all knots and chords, breasts like dead fish hanging in her black canvas suit. Still, she lay there on that flat rock—half in, half out of the water—surrounded by bits of floating kelp and wood chips, unwinding the string of seedy yellow rock weed that was wrapped around her hand.

"Aw Gladdy, don't quit, not yet."

Carl was treading water a hundred feet out, riding the wash of a ferry that had slid into the harbour across the bay.

"Go to hell," she said, and crawled farther up the slope. "I've froze long enough." She rested, breathing heavily, on the sun-coated sandstone shelf of beach.

And just to show how little he cared, he dived under and left her gaping at nothing but heaving surface for so long she was on the verge of whimpering; then came up farther out, laughing. She imagined that even from here she could see the brown snoose stains on his teeth. It wouldn't surprise her if he was chewing now, wouldn't surprise her a bit to see him spit a long brown stream out into the water. The bugger.

"Gettin' old, woman," he yelled. "Your blood's gettin' thin."

And laughed, floating up onto his back. He'd laugh in the Queen's face, that one. Brown teeth showing, and all those lines in his face. Carl Roote had blood as thick and slow as syrup.

"Drop dead," she said, and flopped over to face away from the bay, to face straight into the cliff that rose up 70 or 80 feet, nearly straight up, to home. A path zig-zagged up the slope, through tangled shiny salal brush and oregon grape and blackberry vines, right up past peeling mangey-looking arbutus and scrub oak. From down here the houses were hidden; there might have been nothing at all up there on top but miles and miles of bush.

"Besides," she yelled back over her shoulder. "We got obligations." And rolled her eyes. "A silver engraved invitation. . ." That ought to knock the cheek out of him.

"Shoot."

He swam in and came slapping up out of the water to stand beside her. The black hairs grew right down over his insteps and out onto every toe, to the edge of every thick yellow nail. Dripping water, he grunted and bent to check his watch, which was lying with the sweat-matted socks on his towel.

"A big night," she said. "At least for some."

"Which I sure as hell wish we could miss." He flopped down beside her on the rock. Laid out his big body. The sandstone had been carved by the tides into smooth rolling slabs with granite boulders embedded here and there as if in concrete.

"Well I can't imagine a good enough excuse for *not*

going," Gladdy said, and examined her hands. "Not when you consider." She poked with her finger down into a pocket of trapped water and weeds left behind by the tide. "Not when it's him."

"If one of us drowned."

She gave him a look. "I doubt even then. He never cancelled when the Payne kid—never even made noises about it—and that was only Monday. You'd of thought a thing as horrible as that happening right in the house would put him off but no. An artist is like one of them actors, nothing's important enough to stop the show."

"And when he's your landlord, you're over a barrel," Carl said. He ran his hand down the hair on his chest, flicked the water off in her direction. "Paintings!"

It could have been a curse. Because he knew she wouldn't miss it for the world. "It won't hurt you a bit," she said, "to look at pictures for a while."

"Drowning might be easier," he said. And winked. And sent a stream of brown-gold juice sailing out in an arc to land on a piece of twisted white driftwood.

"Yes." She sat up and rubbed the towel in her hair. "The old lady, Sylvi, says it's the first time he's ever done a one-man show. You wouldn't dare miss it." And dug her fingers in, to dry right down to the scalp. "Now I'll have to set and dry my hair with the electric dryer, you and your ideas."

"It was hot."

"A swim before supper. You'd think we was kids."

He slid a hand in the gaping side of her bathing suit and bounced a breast. "Kids," he said.

"Here!" she said, and slapped at him. "Get your horny paws out!" She looked up the beach to see if anyone was watching. No-one was, no-one ever was. The people along this part of the bay had heated pools up on the top of the cliff, they never came down to the beach. A sailboat, though, was slicing through the water in this direction. "Can't you ever think of nothing else?"

"What else?" he said, and laid one arm across his eyes.

"Go on back in the water," she said, and stood up. "Another dip in that cold will freeze the ideas off of you." Though she couldn't help just a glance at the wet black hairs going down his belly out of sight. Carl Roote was a thick hairy man. Her father had warned her she'd give birth to monkeys with a husband like that, but all they'd ever had was Sparkle, pretty and dainty as anyone could ask for.

"There's only one picture I really want to see at that show," she said, and nudged his ribs with her toe.

He knew. "I'll feel like a goddamn fool." And squirmed.

"At least he never asked you to pose in the nude," she said, and snorting drove her toe into his navel before heading for the trail up the cliff. While he roared at her, she threw a towel-cloth robe over her shoulder and hugged it tight. Let none of them bloody noseys up there gawk at her body. In the water was one thing, but exposed and white in the sun, sagging in great lumps was another. And didn't she know there were eyes at every window? There always were, all along the cliff edge, every house with its eyes watching her appear at the top of the long steep trail and walk across the yard to her own door.

Mediterranean was what some called this place. Visitors gasped, especially at first, and said the place was practically like being in Naples or somewhere. All that cement and those dripping baskets of flowers. The whole bay laid out at the foot of the cliff, blue and shiny in the sun. Ha! She'd Naples them, she said. What it was was a basement suite no matter how you looked at it. The cement patio was cracked and frost-heaved. And how much of the bay could she see from her kitchen window with that bloody big arbutus tree hogging it all? What she'd like to do was take a chain saw

67

to the twisted old bastard and get herself a view to match them that lived above. Trunks was all she saw, big and thick and pink, busting out of their own bark once a year and dropping curled-up skin like parchment scrolls all over her patio.

Though who in his right mind wanted to look across the bay to the spreading suburbs of the city? And farther off, the white stinking smoke from the paper mill?

"Hungry enough yet?" she asked her daughter, who was laid out on a lounge chair reading a magazine.

And the daughter only grunted. Sparkle Roote. Named after that little darling daughter of BO Plenty and Gravel Gerty in Carl's favourite comic strip. Some Sparkle. Gladdy had seen more sparkle in day-old beer, when she was into one of her snits.

It was the Payne kid that put her into the latest. The whole ugly business. It gave you the creeps, that kind of thing always did. And now those two, those Paynes, down at the funeral place, waiting.

Still waiting too, if the silence above meant anything. Not a single footstep had creaked over her head the whole day. No radio playing. No water rushing in the pipes. The middle floor was empty, empty.

Though up top, up in the real house, the A-frame building that sat on them all, old man Wainamoinen would be pacing now, biting his lip over his damn art show, barking orders at the poor stick of a woman he was married to, Sylvi.

Making the supper, Gladdy Roote could almost have sung out loud. Her hair was in rollers now. The new long dress she'd made herself was ironed and hanging from the top of the closet door. Big splashes of red flowers. It must've been, oh ten or twelve years since Carl'd taken her to anything where she had to wear a long dress. He wouldn't be taking her to this either if they hadn't got that silver-engraved invitation for him being a model for one of the paintings. She could just let rip into the loudest song she knew, she was that excited. For Gladdy Roote would rub elbows with the best tonight. Maybe she'd nudge the mayor's wife and say, "That's my old man in that picture there. Lookit the gleam in the bugger's eye!"

Though of course she hadn't seen the painting yet. Not even Carl had seen the thing finished. They'd have to listen to speeches and who knew what all before they could get near it, just like anyone else.

Suddenly, doors slammed above, and footsteps creaked across over her head. The Paynes were home. Gladdy put a hand over her heart, she was scared to think what it meant. She'd tried to avoid them the past two days; people under that kind of strain didn't need nosey neighbours pushing in every time they turned around.

Though she felt, when one set of footsteps went out onto the deck, that it wouldn't hurt a bit to go outside and talk to Sparkle, ask her to help set the table, or ask her if she'd decided yet whether she was going to come along with Carl and her tonight. And discovered, when she did, that just up above their heads, leaning on the railing, was Carrie Payne.

A person had to say hello at a time like that.

Though Carrie Payne, it seemed, would never have noticed if she hadn't. Her eyes were somewhere higher.

"You look tired," Gladdy said.

Well it was true. Why not say it? A young woman like her shouldn't have purple smudges under her eyes.

"We've just come home for a bite to eat," she said. Her hand at her throat.

"Put your feet up," Gladdy said. Get some rest. It must of seemed like the longest day in the world for you.

"Yes. I wouldn't have left but David insisted."

And then, because she just had to: "Anything happened

yet?"

Sparkle's knees slapped together. "Mom!"

Carrie Payne didn't know where to look. Her eyes scurried everywhere looking for something to anchor them.

"No," she said. "No, not yet."

While Sparkle, face red, stomped past into the house. From the door she turned and gave her mother a horrible scowl.

If what you expect really happens, Gladdy thought, the newspaper writers will hound you into an insane asylum: and if it doesn't happen the cops'll lock you in jail. They'll get you one way or the other.

It was the cheekiest she'd been since her operation. She could almost believe she was on the mend. Humming, she went back inside to get the supper out, feeling the huge curls to see if they were dry.

If Eli Wainamoinen were to let go, truly let go, who knew what might happen?

Madness, some people would guess, or greatness. Some, like his wife, thought he had already let go enough and ought to spend a little more time being normal. Wainamoinen himself suspected that he might become one of the immortals, that if he let go altogether and released all the talents swelling within him, he would quite likely soar well above the world of ordinary men and find himself in some kind of timeless place of spirit and harmony.

Not that he despised the world of man and nature.

From his balcony he could see a great deal of it and it was beautiful. Across the top of the arbutus there was the bay-harbour, nearly encircled by the string of beaches and apartments and houses of the town that curled around its edge. The forest too, covering the slopes and reaching up into the harsh gashes in the blue mountains of the island's backbone.

It was a scene he had never painted, or ever wanted to. Too peaceful, too pretty, too pleasant. Art was an act of violence, not a sedative. Each work must begin as an assault on the pure canvas and end as a shock to the viewer's sensibilities. There were harbours in his collection but not this one, not with its comfortable ordinary calm, not where the only colours could be green and white and blue: he preferred the cramped up-island inlets with storm-wrecked docks and crimson boats that bled their reflections into dark water.

He could see the Payne woman on her deck below him. And had seen Gladdy Roote when she came up over the rim of the cliff, panting and hunched over like a sick cow. Two silly women. The incredible thing was that on this of all days it was possible for ordinary people to do ordinary things, completely unaware of how important it was to him, or how frightening. Completely oblivious to the fact that his name, if nothing else, should be enough to give pause on a day like this. You didn't have to ride a viking ship to save the land of heroes. His namesake would have understood that. That there were other ways.

Back home, of course, this day would have come 40 years sooner. But he had chosen, after all, to live here in this country, on this island, where a man had to be 70 years old before he could be sure there'd be people at his first show. They couldn't trust themselves any earlier. How could they be sure he wasn't trying to put one over on them, as they said, until he could show he'd been selling his paintings to art lovers all over the continent for nearly 50 years? Until he could list the museums that bought his work.

And yet, "The people, the people," he said.

And thought of that old composer in Helsinki.

He turned and went back inside the house, his legs aching from tension and the slow hours of pacing. He could be sick, he could easily be sick. But he hadn't waited all these years just to miss out on his own first show. He would be there even if he had a stroke between now and then and had to crawl.

With his wife, his Sylvi.

Sylvi. The perfect wife. Who knew how to protect him. Who stood between him and the people. There were 40 workers getting ready for the show and not once in the two months of preparations had she let a single problem get past her to bother him. He had been able to spend all his time painting.

"Tired, Sylvi," he said. "You look tired." He put both hands on her tiny shoulders and she looked up, grinning, her eyes bright. And tilted her head to let her face rest against his hand. "Eli," she said. And it was clear that she would have crawled through fire to serve. With joy.

"You thought I was saving you from life on a farm, but look. . . look what you have instead. Servant to the selfish one."

Though the farm had been only a cow, and a field on the side of a rocky hill.

"*Mina olen onnellinen*," she said, and kissed the hand.

But he put a finger on her lips. They had agreed: no Finnish, not even in private. They had done everything possible to eliminate any trace of an accent. If he had been Italian, he said, if he had been Spanish or Hungarian or English he would have worked hard to hold onto a foreign accent. It would have been a help to an artist. But not Finnish. A Finnish accent, he said, was something these people expected to hear in the logging camps. A Finnish accent was for fallers and bunkhouse cooks. It could only hurt an artist. It was better even to sound Canadian.

That he used a language of his own they would learn soon enough. In less than two hours.

"Sylvi!" he said and pulled his hand away. "Sylvi! My

warm milk, please now."

"Yes," she said, a gasp. And leapt to her feet. "Yes Eli. And you sit down, in that chair."

"Sit!" He waved his arms at the sloped ceiling. "Don't be a fool, woman. How could I sit?"

Instead he paced the full length of the house, from carved oak door at the front to the sliding glass doors at the rear. Then back. When she handed him the mug of warmed-up milk he looked at it, felt his stomach lift, and gave it back. "Too late, Sylvi, take it away!"

She took the mug and poured the milk down the drain. "Then please stop your marching, Eli, you'll drive the people below crazy."

"Already crazy!" he shouted. The Paynes. Already crazy. "And the bottom floor not much better. You should have seen that woman in her swim suit."

"Hush. Now stop. Calm yourself down. It'll all be over soon. Everything will be well."

They'd stripped the house. There wasn't a painting left on any wall. The workers had come in yesterday and, under Sylvi's direction, had taken down everything he'd painted and hauled it away to the ballroom of the hotel. Even the studio was bare, except for easels and blank canvas and pots of paint.

In Helsinki there'd been such a house. A museum, a composer. It too had been on a cliff overlooking the city harbour. His father had taken him there once, when he was a small boy too young for the composer to notice. He hadn't listened to them talking; instead he'd memorized the house. Every corner, every board, every piece of furniture. And he had reproduced it here, years later, when he knew in his soul that if he'd been back home he'd have far surpassed that composer in the people's hearts. Luckily the builders here were as accustomed to the proper use of wood as they'd been

73

in Finland. And the furniture had been shipped directly from Helsinki. No North American imitation.

He touched it all now. It was something to hold onto. The cedar walls. The thick red carpet. The spiral staircase to their sleeping loft. The lamps. The teak tables. The places where paintings had hung. The door frames at the entrance to his studio.

While the windows in the house had been placed to take advantage of the harbour view, the windows in the studio were arranged for light. Made of a special glass, non-glare and very expensive, they ranged along the north wall, so all the light would be indirect, none of it ever straight from the sun.

"Sylvi! Sylvi!" he called suddenly. "What is all this nonsense I'm doing? A painter should be painting."

"No!" she screeched. But he took off his dress shirt, stripped off the pants of his rented tuxedo.

"My canvas!" he shouted. "My paints!"

So she scurried around him and brought out the easel, set up the first canvas she laid eyes on, set out his paint. "At least you'll be out of the way," she said. . . . "I'll call you when we have only half an hour left."

"Sylvi," he said, when she had almost escaped.

"Yes."

"What will you be doing?"

"My dress, Eli, I have to take it in. I've been so busy I haven't got around to it. It hangs like a sack."

"Never mind." He swung his hands in the air, beating her words away. "Leave the dress. Pray!"

She looked horrified. "What?"

"Go into the bedroom, Sylvi, and pray for me. Pray for the paintings. Pray for the people."

She put her hands to either side of her face. "And you?" she said. "What will you be doing while I'm arranging things with God for you?"

"Working," he said. And drew a blood-red line of paint down the middle of the canvas.

"I don't think He will mind if I talk to Him while I'm using a needle and thread on my dress," she said, and wheeled away. But stopped. "He might even be persuaded to listen to a man holding a paint brush."

"Aggh!" he said, as she slammed the door. And slashed red again, this time horizontally across the white rectangle. Every painting began as a violence against the perfect canvas. You had to understand that every work of art was a violence itself, a cry, a hand slap to wake the hysteric to reality.

He worked, thinking of the people who would be there, at the ballroom, for him.

So long as none of the men were there. If any of the fellows from the maintenance shop showed up he'd clobber that Gladdy for talking him into sitting for that bastard painting. There was no point in hoping nobody who recognized him would come from the paper mill; the bosses would be there, the office men with their white hands, everybody important. Old Wainamoinen knew where the money was in this town.

Carl Roote lay out on his back and floated, looking at sky. A jet going somewhere drew a thin perfect white line that began immediately to drift and shred. Seagulls glided across, screeching. Riding air. Bastard birds, he'd be happy to shoot every one of them, if they let him. If they hadn't made it illegal. As a kid he used to put out food for them on a fish hook attached to plenty of string. Whenever a bird swallowed the food on the hook and flew up level with the tree tops he yanked hard and brought it down.

You had to punish greed. Seagulls would eat anything at all and so asked for what they got. Tourists said Oh aren't they beautiful, so graceful! But Carl thought of the way they hounded you for food, the way they'd gobble up a fish's bloody guts. You had to stomp on gluttony.

He lay out, relaxed, flat on his back. He would lie like this in the back of the family pickup when he was a kid, eyes closed, feeling the wheels beneath taking him steadily toward some place he couldn't see. Relaxed, a sense of motion, surprise. Smelling the dirt and sawdust and rotting leaves that danced around him on the floor of the pickup's bed. You trusted the truck to take you there, you trusted the Old Man to drive safely and quickly and to know where he was going. Just as you knew that if you let go, if you relaxed, the water would hold you up, keep you floating, even when the waves hit.

Then, treading water 100 yards out from shore, he watched the ferry move out of the loading slip and pass silently along the opposite shore, heading for the open strait and the mainland. The waves would be a few minutes crossing the bay, and then they would toss him like a piece of kelp. Behind the ferry the houses in the subdivision were still and quiet in the sunlight; they might have been empty, every one. He could pick out the ones he had built, before. *Carl Roote, Building Contractor*. Before it had become necessary to get the job at the paper mill, in maintenance, patching up other people's rotten work.

Their owners would live in those houses five years, if they were like the others around here, before they moved on to another. The bastards. While Carl Roote rented old Wainamoinen's basement.

He couldn't see the basement from here, but he could see the A-frame top floor standing up above the trees. And through the arbutus he could make out Carrie Payne on the middle floor deck, looking this way. He raised an arm to her, in case she saw, but she made no gesture at all in return.

It was Kit O'Donnell who returned his wave, walking along the beach directly below the house. She was in her bikini, flapping a huge towel in the air. You couldn't help wanting to move in closer, to see. Carl Roote started to swim.

He came out of the water streaming wet, laughing, fingering back his hair. He pulled out the waistband of his trunks to let air inside, to keep the cloth from clinging like a piece of seaweed.

"Well," he said.

And "Well," she said, and spread out her towel on the stone shelf. She lived by herself down in Kennedy's boathouse and could have done her swimming there, but she liked this spot. Fewer crabs, she said, and laughed.

Skinny as a two-by-four but still that bathing suit drew the eyes. Two little pieces of rag. She twisted in the skinny body as if there was another her, inside, separate. And tossed her hair. And spoke with a phony English accent.

She was a teacher. Hardly more than a girl herself, he'd say, but still she was paid to teach teenagers older than Sparkle.

Carl Roote slapped his belly, still hard as it had ever been, though thicker, and danced on his feet on the hot stone. "Mrs. Payne is home," he said.

She looked up the cliff and of course saw nothing. "Oh," she said. Then looked down, at his hairy feet.

"Stupid woman," he said.

"To see God in a bathroom mirror." She put a toe in the water, danced back. He could have counted the ribs; and the small black moles on her back.

"G'on in," he said. "It's a shock at first but you get used of it."

"I saw Gladdy earlier. The two of you were out here like a pair of seals. I couldn't resist coming down. It's wonderful that she hasn't given up swimming."

"Aw Gladdy's gone up, to get supper. She's probably gabbing away with Carrie Payne if I know her at all, or across the fence. That woman would talk to a statue if there was nothing else." He knew his own voice sounded as if he was bragging. As if he had married the only friendly woman in the country. As if nosey was a virtue.

But she didn't dash into the water, or walk in. She crossed her ankles and sat down—folded down—onto her towel, and frowned at a cluster of congregate rocks. "I wonder if it's even possible to imagine what it must feel like to be them right now."

"The Paynes."

She nodded, then threw back her head and scanned the sky. You never knew either what a girl like that was thinking about. Suddenly she slapped her hand on the rock beside her to tell him to sit down.

He did too, and tried to hide his feet down under a cluster of mussel shells and kelp. A crab brushed past his toes and scurried for new cover. "I guess it's not really all that fantastic an idea after all," he said. "My grandmother. . . they figured she was dead once and then she came up and came alive again."

She looked at him. "Really?" She pulled her lips back over her teeth in a way that same speech teacher must have taught her. This was a great town for speech teachers. Kids learned to talk as if they'd been brought up in bloody Buckingham Palace.

So he was conscious of his own voice, flat and rough as a fresh-sawn board. "I was a kid at the time. She got blood poisoning from something, in her hand, in one of the fingers. She died in the hospital, the doctor even sent my grandfather home to break the news. But she revived after that and they had to call him back."

78

She watched him speak, her own lips moving with his, and smiled when he stopped. "Oh but that's different. That's a doctor's stupidity."

"I could hardly stand to be in the same room with her for a long time after that. A big woman, sitting in one corner of her kitchen with that crippled hand in her lap. Like someone who knew something the rest of us had to wait for."

She drew both bony knees right up under her chin. He could see hairs curling out from under the suddenly stretched-tight bikini. "Children," she said, "see things magnified a dozen times. As I believe flies do, or bees."

"So it's not so far-fetched," he said. "And then there's that story in the Bible, that fellow."

She laughed. "Oh but such nonsense has been said about that!" When she said "nonsense" it sounded like a word she'd invented herself, a special velvet word. "Do you think if he believed even for one minute that Lazarus really was dead he'd have been able to raise him up? The only reason he could do it was he knew better than to believe in death at all."

"And so Mrs. Payne?"

"Is fooling herself."

He set his jaw and nodded. Though, somehow, it was a disappointment. You needed a little excitement now and then. Or at least the possibility.

"Anyway," he said, "that's two people won't be there at the old man's show tonight."

"The only people who won't. I heard they used the phone book to make up the guest list."

He snorted. "They didn't waste their time inviting people who can't afford to buy. But that still leaves more people than I want to have finding out I was fool enough to sit and let him paint me."

She put a hand on his knee and laughed, showing him

79

all her teeth. "In the old days mostly they painted royalty. And the nobility." And shook her head at the thought, stirring up her hair. "Count Carl Roote!"

The hand left, went back to join the other in a bridge across the back of her neck. She didn't shave her armpits. That was one thing you'd never find on Gladdy, a single hair or even stubble under her arms. If I wanted to be a European, Gladdy said, you might persuade me to chew garlic but I'd never let my legs and pits become jungles.

"He should of painted Carrie Payne," he said. "Her and her damn mirror!"

She didn't laugh at that. Because of course you couldn't make fun of everything in this world. A few things were beyond that.

So he said, "They're quiet enough people. If you got to have people living on top of you they're good enough. Hardly move, hardly talk. When we lost the house Gladdy didn't know how she could stand living so close to people but she shut up about it when she saw how quiet those two are."

"And their girl."

"Was a friend of our kid's. A nice enough girl. Quiet too until the two of them got alone in a bedroom with a radio. Then watch out."

Then suddenly Kit O'Donnell was on her feet. "Well if I sit here all day talking to you that sun will go down and I'll never get my swim."

And ran in, squealing. On those skinny legs.

Sparkle Roote wouldn't go to the stupid old art show if they paid her. To see a bunch of dumb paintings by that old fart. What was so special about him? Personally she wouldn't walk across the street.

She ate her supper with them all right. There was no

80

way for an only child to avoid that without causing a great big commotion. She tried not to look at her dad, who sat with both arms laid out on the table while he slurped up his macaroni without lifting his hand more than two inches from the plate. In his soiled white undershirt. Black hairs growing on his shoulders. She didn't want to look at her mother either. There was something disgusting about the excitement that flushed up her cheeks, shone in her eyes. She couldn't have stood to see her flouncing around like a lady at that art show. She'd eat her supper with her eyes on the open pages of her book *Lucky at Love* and then she'd play records all night.

There wouldn't be a person left in this building to bother. She could turn the noise up as loud as she wanted. Even the Paynes would be gone again.

She would dream of being a television actress.

Anna Payne had wanted to be a television actress too. First she wanted to be a nurse but they said with her health it was a silly idea. So the two of them had planned to become tall and slender women who slunk and pouted through prize-winning dramas. Anna would get a part in a doctor series, she'd be a television nurse. Sparkle would be a bitch, a sex-goddess, a destroyer of men.

"By then," she said, "you won't need your medicine any more."

But Anna had shaken her head. "I'll always need my medicine. This thing is part of me. I'll have it with me all my life, to the very end. Like a twin, or a lover."

Though other kinds of lovers, too, were important.

Sparkle would sleep with every man that worked for the television company and then pick out the half dozen she wanted to keep with her all the time. Anna would be on the verge of marrying the doctor-star of her show when a wealthy South American would fall in love with her and spirit her away to his plantation where they would live in sin. Whatever that was.

"But isn't eleven too young to be planning these things?" Anna said.

And of course Sparkle, who always knew better, said, "No, you're never too young to plan your life."

The alternative was to end up like Mom and Daddy, or Mr. and Mrs. Payne, or like nearly everyone else they knew.

She wished with all her heart that it was possible for the police to come and take Mr. and Mrs. Payne away to jail and then put nooses around their necks and drop the trap doors open to let them snap dead like a couple of chickens. But that was not possible any more in this country and so she wished that the two of them would be put in a prison until they were old old old and would rather die than come out.

"It wouldn't hurt you a bit to come with us," her mother said.

And her dad: "If *I* have to go..."

She told them she'd rather be tied naked on an ant pile. That shut them up.

It's somewhere in the middle of the week, thought David Payne, but the day escapes me because it doesn't really matter and I'm sitting here at this table beginning to hate my wife. Trying to eat, God help me, trying to bring the fork up coldly, silently with food I don't want and will never be able to keep on my stomach while she stares out that window and waits for me to finish. Like a parent who has taken his child to the bathroom and stands at the door, waiting, looking off somewhere else as if it doesn't matter but really saying with every line of posture and angle of bone, "Hurry up and get your business over with so the more important aspects of life may continue."

David Payne was beginning to hate, more than anything

else, the dark line of tension that creased down the centre of her forehead.

The air in the room was stagnant. All of it tasted second-hand in his mouth, warm and still and slightly sour. She had gone out onto the deck for a while and so a little of the sea air had managed to creep inside but old lady Roote had said something that sent her scurrying back inside to lock the sliding doors. She sat now on the arm of a chair by the window, like a bird ready for immediate flight. Despite the waiting, the days of waiting, the days of sitting and sweating in the heat, her white suit was still impeccable—uncreased, unsoiled, undisturbed.

Her voice, too, was as perfect and cool.

"I have no idea whether that arbutus is a blessing or not. How many people have come in here and said, 'Oh you've got to get them to cut that tree down so you'll have a better view?' But then, the tree itself is our view, isn't it David? It fills up everything and still we can see between some of its branches and watch the swimmers, follow the ferries in and out."

He had no idea what she was getting at. Three days of sitting in a mortuary had made him uninterested in anything she could say. I know what has happened to me and to her and to Anna, he thought, but no amount of sitting in the damn place waiting for something to happen will ever convince me that any of it is real. Because you don't really believe, despite the knowing and the feeling and the way you can see people all around beginning to treat you as if you've suddenly grown an extra skin of mustard yellow, you don't really believe for a moment that it could really have happened to you and that there is nothing you can do to reverse it.

"Remember Aunt Gwennie at Christmas, when she came out from the prairies, she said My word that's a leaf tree but it's still holding onto every one of them at the end of December. You said it's an evergreen despite these big leaves and she didn't believe you. She said evergreen had needles. She said all those pine and firs and hemlocks were hard enough to get used to in the middle of the winter but this, this was some kind of freak. So you had to admit that yes, they did lose their leaves, in July. You told her they went dry and yellow and fell off like big crisp flakes all over the yard. And then you told her the special part: that not one of those leaves fell off the tree until the new ones had already opened up like flower buds on the end of every tiny twig and shone like fake wax leaves in the sun!"

He stood up and carried his plate into the kitchen where he scraped the food off into the garbage container under the sink. Then he carried the other dishes in and put them in the sink. Yesterday's dishes were still piled there, bits of food hardened, turning black. And dishes from the day before. I am an architect, he thought. Within a year I will have built up the healthiest architecture firm in this city and by that time we'll be ready to build ourselves the house we've been dreaming about and planning for a dozen years if the world hasn't fallen in around our ears before then.

Forgetting for the moment that it already had.

He returned to the living-room and saw her from behind. The back of her neck. If you want to know whether you love someone, his mother used to say, then approach her from behind and see what the back of her neck does to you. That is the most vulnerable spot, or seems it, and if you love someone you will want to weep at the knowledge of how vulnerable she is. Why do you think a mother weeps at a wedding? It isn't the music, it isn't the happiness, it isn't even the unhappiness. It's the sight of her son's bare neck turned to her and to life as if to the executioner's axe.

But Carrie's hair was up, swept up, like a girl in a brown

old-fashioned photograph. Even at a time like this she made sure not a hair was out of place. And her neck with that white smooth skin made him think of something someone had laboured over for days and weeks polishing to a perfect shape and shine. Still, though, it was a rigid thing, as marble works of art must be, and not in the least vulnerable.

"Remember how she didn't want to believe about the bark either! How you can hear it on certain days. How the trunk seems to have swollen too big for its casing and so the bark on a hot day snaps and cracks and splits and curls up like scrolls and corkscrews and springs. For an afternoon or two it will sound as if the whole world is rustling old dry newspaper! And there it is, the brand new skin beneath, pale and smooth and already doing all the things a tree's bark is meant to do."

David Payne sat in a chair and put his feet up on a padded stool. There was always the chance she had decided not to go back. There was still the possibility that when she'd stepped inside this small house full of stale air and neglect she realized that all she was doing was wearing herself out and that hope can last only so long.

He really did, David. He really did.

Don't.

An unbelievable light from the mirror. I was blinded. White as snow-glare. And His voice.

Stop it.

Three days. Destroy this temple and in three days I will raise it up. Oh David, David, I know!

He was aware that already there were some who were calling it more than a tragedy. Each time they left the house in their month-old station wagon there were people all down the street who, if this had been another time, another place, would gladly have thrown stones.

I am beginning to hate my wife, thought David Payne.

85

It's somewhere in the middle of the week but the day escapes me because it doesn't matter and I'm sitting here beginning to hate my wife. At a time when she needs to be loved, God help me, more than at any other time in her life.

"The others will be right across the street from the. . . from the place," she said. "At the art show. When it happens they'll be right there, they'll be the first to know. After us."

She looked at him for the first time since they'd come home. Her eyes, her pale face, were as rigid and polished as her neck. There was not a flush of doubt. Not a flicker of vulnerability.

I am beginning to hate this woman, thought David Payne. And discovered that already he was crying.

Carl was in one of his moods.

He'd started out by drinking three beers before supper and another two with it, despite her warning. You couldn't go to a thing like this smelling like a brewery. But he'd got glummer and poutier and redder and had barked at them both so much the kid finally got up and stomped into her bedroom.

And now he was trying to get friendly. Drying dishes beside her, for Pete's sake, something he never did. Sliding hands inside her dress. Saying let's forget the show Gladdy and head for the bed. Kissing her neck with the old whisker bristles scratching. "Get away," she said, and side-stepped, but he kept up until she threatened him with two soapy hands.

"Shoot," he said. "What fun is it?"

Gladdy would easily spend the whole day in bed with Carl. He was that much fun sometimes. But not when he was drinking. She'd more than once stayed in bed with him through a whole Saturday, when Sparkle was away staying at a friend's and it was more fun than anything, but never when he'd been drinking. Beer made him stink. She hated the smell until she'd had some herself. And it made him useless in bed, all he wanted to do was paw her and tickle her and get her all worked up without any hope of relief.

Though on his good days he could make that bed rock. The first week they were married they brought it crashing down off its legs. Carl could bring a barn down if he tried. They left the bed where it lay, on the floor, solid and quieter than some squeaky thing up on flimsy legs.

But when he got a few in him he couldn't have got a hammock swaying.

That was the first thing he told her about himself, when they met at a dull party thrown by a friend. She was hardly twenty then, working in Eaton's office. "I can keep it up all night if I'm sober, I can outlast an elephant. But put a few drinks in me and I'm useless." She told him she'd take his word for it thank you but she knew from her first look at those long-boned thick hairy hands that she'd be finding out for herself soon enough. She fell in love with his thick, cracked chewed-down fingernails. His left thumbnail was black, dead, ready to fall off.

Some people thought she could've done better. "Better than what?" she said. "He's a carpenter, a contractor. There's money in real estate." But he spends it as fast as he makes it, they said, on pleasure. On useless tasteless things, just to squander it. "He loves me," she told them. "He's crazy about me." And they had only been able to cry that oh, but he was so red and hairy!

That was what bothered them the most. A man who looks like that, a man who can't keep his hands off you even in public! More animal than human. Some day he'll turn on you like a mad dog. But she had liked the attention he paid. To feel his hand going up the back of her leg while

87

she was talking to someone. To have his hands inside her clothes while she was on the phone. To have him surprise her from behind when she was at the sink. Animal shmani-mal, they could have their bloody gentlemen with manners. She liked to be lusted after. She liked to have him keep every nerve in her body tingling with life, keep all of her alive and guessing. With Carl around there was never any question what she was.

Even when his business went belly-up, even when they lost the house and he was feeling so bad, he never stopped wanting her. Or making her feel like she was the most im-portant thing to him. That was the one thing that didn't change in their life. He was as randy as ever. Not even her operation slowed him down, except out of respect when she was overwhelmed sometimes by a huge tiredness.

Though there were times, like now, when it wouldn't seem right anyway. Not when she was about to dress up like a real lady and go to a high-class do. It was bad enough he got her into the ocean, ruined her hair when it was too late to do much but dry it and slap on one of her wigs. She wasn't going to let him breathe his beery breath all over her. Or keep her from a nice hot bath.

Over their heads a floorboard creaked.

"Not gone back yet," she said, and plunged her hands into water.

"You think the police?"

She closed her eyes, nodded. "Must be waiting just to be polite. One thing about the Mounties, sometimes they're not as crude as you expect police. They're just waiting for today to be over, so's everyone can see what a fake."

"Still, if it happens."

"It won't happen, hush up."

"Still, if it does."

"If it does you won't see my ass for dust. You won't see

this old girl. I'd be scared to ever put my foot in this house again."

"But if it does, just think."

"Think nothing." She threw him a scowl. "You must be geting soft in the head." And tossed a whole handful of wet soapy cutlery onto the rack for him. "Can't you tell a couple of loonies?"

Carl chuckled. Sucked air through his teeth. He always did when she got arched, when the colour rose in her face and her voice strained.

Though he knew it only made her worse.

She stomped a foot. Tied here to the sink by dripping hands, she would like to have stomped out on him. The way Sparkle did. But he sucked air through the spaces in his teeth, laughing at her, and put one hand on her rump.

"Off!" she said, and swung her hip.

And "Off!" again, because it held on like a huge suction cup. She danced sideways, trying to lose him. But he held on, laughing, and put the other hand there too, on the other side, and squeezed.

"Bastard!" She brought up the hands, red and dripping with soap bubbles, and swung on him. He tried to get a kiss down into her throat but she pushed both palms into his face and fanned them like windshield wipers to cover it all.

"Ha!" she cried. "How do you like that?"

He didn't. Not at all.

"Jesus, Gladdy." And stepped back just long enough to finger soap off his eyelids. And look at her as if he was considering. A fist perhaps: he'd hit her before now, it wouldn't be the first time. He hated to be pushed away, he always hit back. Bent over like that, his legs apart, she would have believed it to see him charge at her like a bull and drive his head into her stomach. That too, had happened before.

And still, she was glad she had done it. She picked up the

89

dishtowel he'd dropped, wiped both hands dry on it, and dropped it on the counter. "It's time for my bath," she said, and dared him with her eyes to stop her. "I'll just have time to get dressed. Your suit's pressed and hanging."

"Pressed and hanging," he said. "Screw the suit. If you think I'm going to that stinkin' affair."

"Go or not, please yourself,' she said. "It don't make any difference to me. *I'll* be there."

But he blocked her escape. "Look Gladdy, I don't want to go to that bastard affair. What the hell business have I got in a place like that?"

Upstairs, the floorboards creaked again. Footsteps passed over.

"No business at all if you think of it that way," she said. "But if you don't go you'll sit here and worry your gut out thinking about all those people seeing your picture. You may as well be there to look too. Sylvi told me the price on it would be $800."

"What?" he said, grinning despite himself. "$800 for this mug? Who's gonna pay that?"

"Somebody with money to burn," she said. "Somebody who'll put it in the basement to scare the rats away."

"Huh."

"Maybe your ugly face will hang in a gallery somewhere. For tourists to gawk at. They might even charge admission for the pleasure." She cocked her hip at him and walked past. Then turned. "You and the bloody Mona Lisa."

He lunged for her but she stepped aside and all he got ahold of was the collar of her dress. But he yanked on it anyway, sent buttons flying, ripped the seam open. "God damn!" she shouted, and slapped at the arm. But he pulled harder, and tore a strip right down the front. An old housedress but one of her favourites. "You son of a bitch."

He was sucking air again, through his teeth, but his face

was red with anger. No-one laughed at Carl Roote. Not if he didn't want a poke, or the hard thrust of a shoulder.

But she knew how to handle that. She put both hands on her stomach and grimaced. Groaned.

"Gladdy?"

She hunched across to the nearest chair and sat. Carefully.

"Is it the operation?"

She nodded. And indeed, now, she could feel the pain there. Throbbing. She put up her hand and he took it, held it tight.

She didn't even have to use her magic word, it was that easy this time. Sometimes she had to haul out the word the doctor had given her like a weapon and fling it at him to stop him dead. Hiss it at him. Make him leap back and turn away. But this time just the few groans, the doubling over, were enough.

"Aw Gladdy, are you all right?"

She was all right, yes. She nodded. And watched him. He was sober enough now. She'd scared the beer right out of him. Look at those eyes.

"All right," he said. "We'll go. You get that dress on and we'll go to their bastard art show."

She put her hand on his arm. The pain was worse, which served her right for conjuring it up in the first place. "Go get your suit on, you dumb ox," she said. "I've still got the time for a quick bath."

It was true that Sylvi Wainamoinen spent a great deal of her time dreaming of pilgrims. They came to her door, in her dreams, wide-eyed and afraid. They came down to the door from their cars, from the tourist buses, from their taxis, they came whispering across the gravel on tip-toe as if what they walked on was holy ground, they came from all over the island, from all over the country, from all over

91

the world, with breaths held and hands tight: just to see her, to see her home, to touch her things.

So she dreamed.

Oh, she was willing to admit it. To herself, and to Aili too, soft sweet almost forgotten Aili, momma, who smelled of the dairy and cinnamon cookies. Who lived, now, like the pilgrims, only in her dreams.

She opened the door to them, she confessed, in the black rags of widowhood.

It was true, certainly, that she was spending larger and larger portions of her days on the dreams, but it had never before occurred to her that when the time came for at least part of it to come true she would be too tired to care. That her cheeks would burn from lack of sleep, that her arms would ache, her eyelids droop.

Yet she was expected to be a gracious hostess, once they got to this thing. The helpers would all turn to her for advice; she'd be expected to make it all run smoothly. And what did she know of such things? Really? Why were there helpers at all if everything, everything must be told to her?

She would be expected to check everything over. The paintings, were they straight? Were the helpers in their places? Were the programs out? The price list posted on the walls in several places? Eli would be up on the platform with the alderman, ready for the people. She could go home at that point, if she wanted, and it wouldn't really make that much difference. Except of course to Eli. Except to insult him.

She played with her wedding ring. Plain gold. A ring was a reminder that eternity was not impossible, he'd told her, that some things could go on and on so that you couldn't tell beginnings from endings. A marriage was supposed to be like that.

There were 250 paintings. A lifetime, hanging on those

walls, and on the standing screens. Some were new, hardly dry. Half of them were borrowed from the owners. She could stand there in the centre of that hall and, by turning slowly all the way around, follow the 75 years of her husband's life.

And could, even if he himself disappeared. His life was broken up, reflected, mirrored in these 250 rectangles. Those people out there would see nearly as much of him as she'd ever seen. If he'd welcomed them naked he'd be no more exposed than he was already.

Back home they would say, *"Miksi Sina olet nun hidas."* What took you so long? Here there were some who said, "Are you sure you're ready?" and "Is there any point? When you know that few really care?"

"Aili," she whispered, "can I confess you something once again?"

I dream of myself welcoming pilgrims, travellers who have come from all parts of the world to our house, which has become a shrine. "You," they say with emotion that closes the throat. "You are the widow? You knew the Wainamoinen? You lived with him all those years?" The house is owned by the government as a museum (can you imagine that?) and I show them through the studio, show them the unfinished canvases, let them touch the furniture in our home.

It will be easier then, Aili, much easier. Of course I never expected any of it to be simple, living with him, but oh, so much of it has been hard.

"Oh you silly fool baby," Aili would laugh at her. "You dreamer baby. Do you really believe it's any easier for the rest of us? Can you imagine you're the only one who wants to be a widow?"

"Sylvi!"

It was Eli, calling her from the open door. Outside, she

could hear the car's motor running. "Get your coat on, Sylvi. It's time to go."

"Yes," she said. "Yes." And touched the hair at the back of her neck.

"Before we go," David Payne said, "we should stop in upstairs and wish them luck."

"Luck?" she said, and raised a perfect eyebrow. "What would a thing like that mean, coming from us?"

"Still," he said.

She smiled. "To wish good fortune for someone else you should at least have demonstrated a little of it yourself."

So if there was no doubt in her, he thought, there was at least some bitterness. Waiting was a strain, even waiting for something you were so sure of.

He turned on the radio. "We'll go, just as soon as I've heard the news," he said. And sat back in his leather arm chair in the corner. "If you insist on taking me back to that place."

There were ten minutes left, however, before any of the stations would be offering news and all he could find was music. He snapped off the switch.   What kind of a union is it that falls apart this easily, he thought. Where was its strength if it could hold together through all the first twelve years of growing and planning and learning and then snap like this from the weight of its first real burden? What was the matter with him?

"If you really believed," he said, "you'd be full of joy and excitement."

She did not look at him. She spoke with her face turned away, in the direction of the window, the arbutus tree, the harbour. "Who are you to know what believing brings with it?"

Wainamoinen sat back on his chair and crossed one leg

94

over the other. Perfectly, carefully. No-one must see an old man slouched down like a pouting child dragged here by his parents. Nor see bare white leg exposed above the stocking. This was a time for dignity.

And it was too late to do anything about the red smear of paint along the side of his hand. Except to hide it, for now, in the left pocket of his suit.

As people entered the ballroom, nervously, tentatively, he tipped back his head and closed his eyes. Now, now it was happening.

Only One
Life of us all
open my eyes
only to perfection,
mine
and theirs

Why, why, they said, did you choose to hide yourself on that island? Frontier island on the far edge of a frontier country. When you could have had Scandinavia first and then Europe and finally all of the world. In a country that is only beginning to care you hide out on an island that is not yet even aware of itself.

It was because this island was a big enough country, he told them. If he were an Irishman he'd have a country not very much bigger and it would be enough, more than enough. In Finland too, the country is small and yet as big as one man can identify with. Insist that he become a Canadian painter, or a North American painter, and he would panic. How was it possible to identify with anything so unimaginably huge except by induction, except by seeing the small first and knowing it so well it must include all of the rest?

Should he be like his son, who had gone south to America? To become a famous movie director. Who ever heard of him? What could he show that country of itself that they hadn't had to show him first? Robert Arfie Wainamoinen, big shot.

Caroline, on the other hand, had married a mechanic and moved up-island to help him run a broken-down crossroad service station. She was poor and bone-tired from bringing up those kids in a pile of discarded car parts but she knew every inch of that piece of land and could sing of it so that you'd think she'd seen the backyard of every wife in the world.

Only One
Life of us all
open my eyes
only to perfection

What he opened his eyes to was a crowd of hushed people filling up the room, moving in close to the platform. Faces looked up at him. Frozen uncertain smiles. They might have been saying: Are you sure there is no catch to this? Are we really here for what we think we are here for? They moved in, more and more of them, closer gradually to the platform. Standing uncertain, then pushed ahead by still more coming in, then standing again. Waiting.

Their eyes flickered across him, briefly, and strained to see all they could of the paintings around the outside walls of the ballroom. Trying to look as if they were only casually interested. Men, some men, gathered in clusters and spoke agitatedly, about work perhaps, or about politics, certainly not about him; they probably weren't even quite sure why they were here, had been dragged here by their wives. Some wouldn't even be certain of his name.

There was still the red smear on his hand, which he kept hidden. This was not a crowd that wanted an eccentric. They would hate him enough for the platform, for the speeches. Age and dignity and quiet calm were closer to what was expected. An artist who was normal, who wouldn't try to cheat, who wouldn't be tempted to make a fool of you. They wanted to know that if they liked a piece of work there wasn't somewhere behind it the kind of artist who was laughing, thinking: Fool, fool, it's a piece of junk, I wiped my brushes clean on it!

What they wanted of course was not an artist at all but rather a kindly trustworthy art teacher. Dull and gentle. No affectations. Well, he could be gentle.

As his son, too, had been gentle. "My God, dad, they're all a bunch of raving lunatics down here! They call me the dull Canadian." The dull Canadian of course, had become even duller when faced with a public that expected madness. And so eventually, he must have faded right out, respectable and grey and unnoticed. In less than five years.

Sylvi closed the door, then opened it again just long enough to let in one more alarmed-looking woman from the foyer.

Then silence. At the other end of the platform the alderman stood up behind the microphone.

Ladies and gentlemen...

Most of them watched the alderman. A few, still, were looking at the paintings. Gladdy Roote was grinning at him. As if out of all this crowd she thought she was the one he'd be happiest to see! The silly woman; a cow in the parlour.

Which was hardly what he could call seeing only perfection.

The truth was, he knew, that she was probably getting more enjoyment out of this thing than anyone else. Including him. Including even Sylvi. She just didn't have the others' ability to hide it. Poor simple silly woman. She may be the only one in the room who truly loved living.

. . . who took his training under the very best teachers. . .

And Carl, who knew how to suffer. Red and sweating. Trying to look invisible. Hoping no-one would notice his fingers prying the tight collar away from his neck. His coarse hard face clamped shut, his eyes shifting.

"Never mind, Carl," he thought, "when you see what I've done with that face you'll forget your discomfort. You'll see yourself for the first time from the outside."

. . . moved with his lovely wife to this island. . .

It was a face he had known for nearly five years that he must paint some day. From the day they came to look at the basement suite. And yet it had been necessary to wait all that time, watching, thinking, planning, before even asking the man. So that when the time came it had been possible simply to put down what he had already done in his mind. With Carl sitting, of course, so the light would be right.

His son had lived in the basement. Robert, with that Chinese girl. For nearly two years. A trial marriage, they called it. And Sylvi, poor Sylvi, had said at least they'll be home, they're not sneaking off somewhere, we can keep an eye on them. But the Chinese girl had gone and soon after that Robert had gone too—off to Hollywood to become a famous director—and then the Rootes had arrived to answer the FOR RENT ad in the local paper.

. . . fortunate for all of us that such a man should choose. . .

"We saw your ad," Carl said. He made it sound as if he were accusing them of a crime.

"A basement suite?" Gladdy said. Looking around the place. Sniffing the air, perhaps, for flower scents and the odours of dogs. She was ordinary, an ordinary heavy sagging woman, an ordinary face. He would quickly have forgotten her face if they'd never come back.

But he could not have forgotten Carl's. Not ever. His was a face that would have to be painted sooner or later. Those scowling eyes, like velvet blackberries. The bone-stretched jaw, the skin creases. The sudden thick nose. The way a tiniest movement of any part changed all of it, as if the light had changed, or a mask had shifted.

"Well, can you show it to us?" he asked. It was obvious he didn't really want to rent, not this or any other place. "We musta been through a dozen of these bastard places."

Gladdy had explained, almost in a whisper, that they had lost their house, that the business had gone bankrupt. And Carl had told her to shut up, never mind telling everybody all your goddamn business. Though they had clung to each other the whole time as if they were afraid that any minute one of them would turn a corner and disappear.

...ladies and gentlemen, Elias Wainamoinen...

He rose (one leg had gone to sleep) and walked carefully to the mike. Head high. Aware of the heavy silence.

Forty years.

"My friends," he said.

Though he saw none of them. He spoke to the far corner of the ceiling.

"My good friends. Around you, on every side of you, is the evidence of my career."

Sylvi was there; there was Sylvi; standing by the door. Her face tilted; flushed. She was tired.

"Perhaps a man's life is a journey toward heaven."

He paused, closed his eyes.

"Perhaps some people from time to time achieve moments there. Perhaps an artist is the man who can show you glimpses of those moments."

He breathed deeply, tilted forward now, almost bowing. "Thank you for coming, my friends. I hope, this evening, some time this evening, my work will give you a glimpse

99

into the harmonious world of truth."

Not offering much is he, Gladdy thought. The harmonious world of truth for crying out loud!

And shifted weight in her tight shoes. She hadn't worn the things since winter. So much barefoot walking in summer had spread out her feet.

The dress, though, the dress was perfect. Hung on her body like it was made in Paris for her. She looked as good as any one of these other babes, anyone could see that at a glance.

She felt flushed from excitement, but didn't look as red as Carl. The poor bugger hated to wear a suit and tie anyway, and here he was with his head the colour of a fat radish, and sweating buckets as if that collar was really squeezing. His eyes bulged. And never stopped peering around the room the whole time the speeches were on, searching for the shock of his own face looking back.

"You'd think he was a bloody Michaelangelo," she whispered, out of the side of her mouth, to Carl. And nodded, smiling, at the woman who turned to let a look scorch right down the full length of Gladdy Roote.

Your face's got as much paint slapped on it as some of these canvases, Gladdy thought. And wondered if the necklace was real diamonds. In this town, who could tell?

Mercifully the ribbon was cut at last and the crowd fell apart like struck billiard balls. They spread out in every direction all over the hall, running—some of them—to get a closer look at something their eyes had picked out while they stood listening. Someone, moving, kicked Gladdy's ankle; though she swallowed the curse that rose in her throat, and smiled. This aint a bloody $1.49 day at Eaton's, she thought. Were the rich at an art show like housewives at a bargain sale?

"Where's the picture?" Carl muttered. So we can get the hell out of this place."

But no-one was going to cheat her out of one minute of this

"You can't just look and go."

He mopped his high shiny forehead with his handkerchief and glowered. "What else are we here for?"

"You gotta mix," she said.

"Mix?"

"This isn't a department store. You gotta look at every painting like it was the only one here, and you gotta talk with people."

"Shoot, I'm not looking at 250 goddam pictures. And we don't know any of these people."

She slipped her hand in behind his elbow. "We know some. Enough." And smiled at her dentist's second wife, who had begun, after all, as his receptionist. "We'll start here," she said, "and work our way around."

Down the first wall there wasn't a single painting she'd say thank you for. Not one she'd have in her house. A photograph cut out of a magazine would look better than any of these. A lot of trees with fuzzy leaves, and silly messed-up skies. Carl pulled her down past them too fast to see anything else but she didn't mind. What she minded was not having the time to get a good look at the people who stood there, studying. They seemed to be saying things about the paintings as if one wasn't the same as the next.

"Did you notice the prices he's got on these things?" Carl said.

"Paintings are a good investment."

"How much do you figure he pays for the canvas? Not much. And the paint. He sure as hell puts a high price on his labour."

"What else is there to a painting but the labour? You

don't think these people came here to admire the paint, do you? Or the frames?"

Carl Roote shook his head. You'd think he was looking at the biggest con job of all time. Still, he wasn't going to spoil *her* night. Gladdy stood back from a large watercolour in the corner and tilted her head. "Now that's got depth," she said.

The fat woman beside her smiled. "Yes," she said. "That man understands light."

"Yeah," Gladdy said. "You could guess exactly what time of day it is, where the sun's coming from."

The woman moved up closer, one pudgy finger out, as if she wanted to touch.

Carl said, "Maybe he knows light, but he don't know nothing about a logging claim. Them trees are all too clean and perfect. Where's the dead limbs? Where's the rotten snags and widow-makers? Where's the windfalls?"

The fat woman looked Carl over. "Have you met this, this Mr. Wainamoinen?"

"Oh yes," Gladdy said. "We know him well. Neighbours. I suppose we're what you could call friends."

The woman's face lighted up. "Really! Well he certainly is a talented man."

"My husband," Gladdy said, "modelled for him."

Carl growled. The woman's eyes darted to him, away, then back again. Clearly she didn't believe.

"We haven't seen the picture yet," Gladdy said. "We don't even know if it's a good likeness."

"Shoot," Carl said. "Let's get. . ."

"It's the first time I ever heard of a Finn who could paint," the lady said. "They don't go in for things like this. As a rule."

"Mr. Wainamoinen," Gladdy said, "has always painted."

Which ended that conversation. The fat woman tip-toed

on to the next painting as if she were really invisible and had only to be silent to be undetected. As if paintings were things to sneak up on, like whispering children.

"Aw Gladdy," Carl said. "Let's see that damn thing and get out of here. I'm dry as hell." He ran a finger around the inside of his collar. "A beer would help."

"There's a cocktail lounge next door," she said. "We could step in for a drink once we've seen it." She could have promised him anything then, her heart was so full. This was where she belonged. Always she had known this was the kind of do she could fit into. She could sing, she could stay forever, she could promise Carl the moon out of pure joy.

"If we go out to the middle of the room and turn around we should be able to pick it out," he said.

"In this crowd?"

"Over their heads. I'll stand on your shoulders if I have to." And put a hand on her breast. Hidden fish. For reassurance, perhaps, or gratitude.

She stepped back, looking for people who'd seen. No-one had. And anyway, when she did that, he moved his hand to her rear end and bent down to whisper in her ear. "Where's the nudes?"

"The what?"

"There's bound to be some naked bodies in a few of them. All them artists get naked girls to model for them."

"Speaking of naked," she said, and watched Kit O'Donnell slither by in something scarlet and see-through and nearly indecent. Then she said, "Mr. Wainamoinen don't do that kind. People's heads and hillsides are his specialty. I don't expect you'll find a single nude here."

They worked their way out to the centre of the room. Carl stood up on his toes and strained to find his portrait over people's heads but he felt silly and gave it up. "We could be stuck here all night," he growled. And would have started making his way to the door if Gladdy hadn't spotted Wainamoinen himself coming toward them, his arms outstretched like she was a sister he hadn't seen in twenty years.

"Gladdy," he said, and put one hand on her shoulder. "Carl," and put the other hand on Carl's arm. He looked at one and then the other. "These people," he said, and held out both hands like someone feeling for rain. "These people, they fill me with something, with. . ." and one hand slapped back onto his own chest, unable to grasp the perfect word.

"A good-sized crowd," Gladdy said. He must've been a handsome man at one time, she thought. One of those strong slant-boned Finnish faces. With eyes that moved like glittering birds. And white even teeth that slanted in, with spaces. He was a tall man, with big thick hands that could just as easily have held a chain-saw as a brush all these years. "Yes," she said. "You never know."

"Eh?" Carl said.

"Art lovers," Gladdy said, raising her voice. The noise of people talking around them seemed to be getting louder. "You don't have to be rich to like pictures!" And straightened out Carl's red-and-green plaid tie that had got somehow crooked. From all his fingering at it probably. He couldn't keep his hands off a tie once it started bothering his neck.

"This town," Wainamoinen said, "has truly turned out to honour an old man. And to see if my hand has captured more truth than their eyes have seen." He tilted his head back and looked around. "Look well, my friends. I offer you more of the real world in this room than you may see in a lifetime of looking at cars and houses and streets and at the daily monotony of your jobs."

"I wondered if you would have music," Gladdy said. "But in this crowd, no-one would've heard a note. Listen to them."

104

Then, suddenly Sylvi was at her husband's side. She dipped her head in a dry nod to Carl, to Gladdy.

Thinks she's his bloody watchdog. Deciding who's good enough to talk to her precious husband.

"You look lovely," Gladdy said. "Sylvi."

"And you," she said. Sweetly smiling, her dimples deepening. In Finland she would probably have become a factory worker. Tightening nuts. Tittering behind her hand in the lunch room.

"A big night," Gladdy said. "You must've had your picture taken a hundred times for the papers already."

Again the dimples, though the eyes remained flat and dull. "Not of me," she said. "It's Eli's night. His alone."

"Sylvi," the old man said, and put an arm across her shoulder, pulling her close.

"Of course," Gladdy said. "But you too. You must be proud."

"I'm happy at least two of our neighbours could come," said Sylvi Wainamoinen. "Because of course the Paynes." And smiled, sadly.

Gladdy lowered her eyes, she hoped enough. "A tragedy."

Though Carl, the bugger, didn't know when to keep quiet. "Closer than you think," he said. "That funeral place is right across the road. Where they're waiting."

The old man looked frightened. A rosy flush burned at the edges of his eyes. "Hysteria," he said. "Stupid emotional people."

It was clear his wife agreed. Her hand went to his, clasped it. "The woman is clearly unwell, I feel sorry for the husband. Sitting waiting in that morbid place. And who could have known ahead of time?"

"Still," Carl said. "There is still the chance she's right."

Wainamoinen's eyebrows dropped like two grey wings. "Carl," he said. And looked away. "But you haven't said if you've seen the portrait."

"No," Gladdy said, quickly. "Not yet." And would happily have disappeared.

"No. 97," Sylvi Wainamoinen said, lifting a finger vaguely to her left.

The old man beamed. "At least five people!" he said. "Five people or more have shown interest. The painting will be sold before this evening is through. A beautiful thing, Carl, it's one of my best. A beautiful thing."

"Eli," his wife cautioned.

"Yes, one of my best. And the title, Carl. Do you know what the title is?"

If it says Carl Roote on it we may as well pack up right now, Gladdy thought. He would never stand for that.

But no. The old man lifted those eyebrows once again. "You'll see, I've made you immortal."

And so, suddenly, she and Carl were left standing in the middle of the room. Her bloody feet hurting. People's cigarette smoke stinging her eyes.

"C'mon," Carl growled at her. "Let's get this goddamn thing over with." He elbowed a stoop-shouldered man out of the way.

David Payne, driving his car up through the web of downtown streets with his wife beside him silent and white and rigid with both hands fisted together before her mouth, wished for two things: that his day would be over as quickly as possible, and that whatever was going to happen after that would happen swiftly and with little trouble. He did not bother wishing that the dull pain in every bone of his body should go quickly or that the faint dizziness in his head should pass: such things were unimportant and would leave him anyway once this other business was over.

Wednesday. That's what it was, Wednesday. The streets

were deserted, or nearly. A few people walking toward the theatre. It had been Monday morning, he'd barely settled into work at the office, when they phoned from the hospital to say it was too late, by the time they got the girl into the hospital it was too late for anyone to help her, that she had died quietly without ever regaining consciousness; and he had said, "What? What? What are you talking about? Are you talking about my daughter? Anna's at home, she was still sleeping when I left." They told him he'd better get over right away because obviously he'd been under the wrong impression and had better talk with his wife too who was sitting on a couch right there, right beside the phone. Where she was still sitting when he got there and hurled himself across the waiting room toward her and shouted out, "What's going on?" She sat, unruffled, undisturbed—he would have said uninvolved—and said Anna was dead but don't worry because she'd been promised something in three days. He said, "What?" and she said, "He promised. Destroy this temple and in three days I will raise it up."

"Don't be afraid, David," she said. Her hands, her beautiful hands, were folded like soft white petals in her lap. "You mustn't be afraid."

"Waiting for what?" he said. "We've never been inside any kind of a church since the day we were married. We know nothing of God. I can't recall you ever admitting even that you prayed. Who are we to expect a miracle?"

She'd looked at him as if he were a new, only slightly interesting piece of furniture someone had moved in front of her.

"There are people who refuse to believe in death," he said. "But they have their reasons and I don't pretend to understand them. There are even people who have cured people of hopeless diseases and brought them back from the edge of the grave through the power of prayer. I've read of them. But they have their reasons, they know what they're doing, they claim to understand what God is all about."

She crossed one leg over the other and closed her eyes while she pressed two fingers into the furrows of her forehead. She always looked, wherever she was sitting, like a person who was installed permanently in the chair. Or waiting for it to take her wherever it was she wanted to go.

"They don't just hope," he said. "They don't just have faith. They have reasons."

But she too had her reasons, she told him at last. The mirror, the voice, the promise.

As she had always had reasons, for everything she did. For marrying him in the first place: she was an interior decorator and it was just as easy to fall in love with an architect as with anyone else, she said, and much more practical. For insisting on living in rented suites all the twelve years of their marriage while every one of their friends had bought at least one house: she couldn't see any point in settling into anything of their own until they could afford the dream house they were capable of creating together. For refusing even to consider a second child once they'd discovered what was wrong with Anna: "Can you imagine what it would be like for her to have a *perfect* sister, a *perfect* brother?" she said, and shuddered at the thought as if only a monster would consider it. For heading off at least once a year with the girl to some different part of the continent seeking out every hint of a possible cure; she believed that any doctor who practised on this island couldn't possibly know all the latest discoveries and inventions, and any parent who didn't at least investigate all the possibilities no matter how remote was cheating his own child out of a normal life and ignoring his first duty.

He drove along the harbour where tourists in their yachts stood talking across the floats to one another, over the still oily water. Then up through town and on up the hill. He would like to press his foot right to the floor, keep right on going up the hill, off up the mountain, into nowhere, into somewhere else. But he drove—carefully, because here, suddenly, cars full of young people were racing from light to light—on up through town and onto the short street to the mortuary. For blocks ahead the street was lined on either side with cars, a surprise at first until he remembered that this was Eli Wainamoinen's night, his show. "In another country this would have happened 40 years ago," Sylvi Wainamoinen had told him. "But here, we must wait until a life is almost over before we dare to celebrate it." David Payne couldn't see how a gathering of a few hundred people on Vancouver Island could be called celebrating a life, but then he had never pretended to understand what the business of art and artists was all about.

As he pulled up in front of the Blessed Sleep Funeral Home and parked his car in the reserved area, someone opened the door to go into the ballroom of the hotel across the street. Light slid out across the blacktop parking lot like a sudden thrust finger when the door opened, then pulled back in again and died suddenly. "It would be polite to at least put in an appearance," he said, though he would rather walk naked into fire than step in front of all those eyes.

And she did not disappoint him. She breathed in, heavily. "No," she said, and exhaled. "Nobody would expect."

You could've stolen the show, he thought. Who'd want to look at a lot of old-man paintings when there's an honest-to-goodness fanatic in your midst? Wainamoinen would gnash his teeth in jealousy, and Sylvi—poor Sylvi—would have our furniture out on the street by the time we got home again.

Oh how nice to see you, Mrs. Payne, and isn't this the day your little girl?

Yes, yes, but not a flicker yet.

Well never mind, the night's still young. I love your suit.

Dear God, he thought, and suddenly yanked on the hand brake. A police car moved slowly down the street and until it had gone out of sight the weight of pain on his chest nearly broke him.

He cracked all the finger joints of his left hand, one after the other. Then he did the same thing with the right.

"This is it," he said.

But she didn't move. "It's not as if I actually *did* something," she said. "It's not as if I hurt her."

"Or anybody else," he said. And hung his head. "Poor Carrie, you never hurt anybody in your life."

She did not move.

"Sometimes," he said, "in a particularly rainy spring the parent birds will let their children starve to death while they hover over them trying to keep them dry."

She looked at him. "Because they're afraid," she said. Then she said, "Let's go. Charlie will be wondering what happened to us."

Lost her, damn it. He'd gone and lost her. You couldn't take ten steps in this bastard crowd without your wife disappearing. People buzzed around like somebody was stirring them with a stick, the bottom of a paint can.

He would rather have been at home, where there was no-one who pushed and shoved. He would rather have been back in the water again, cold as it would be by now, just lying out on his back and floating. You could trust the water, it would hold you up if you let go and allowed it. You could lie on your back and feel all of it below holding you up while you kept your eyes on the sky or closed them to watch your own dreams. You couldn't trust a crowd like that, it would even swallow your own wife.

He would have left her entirely, gone right out the door and waited for her somewhere in the foyer or downstairs in the beer parlour if it hadn't been for Kit O'Donnell.

"Carl!" she said, and broke loose from the crowd. "You look like somebody's lost little boy. Ready to cry!"

"Arrrgh," he said, and started to stomp out.

But she stood in front of him, head swivelling on that skinny neck. "Where's Gladdy? You always seem to have just misplaced her."

"Lost her," he said. "She was with me, and all of a sudden she wasn't. We was headed for the picture."

She put her finger to her lip, considered. "The place is full of booby-traps," she said, and spilled a small chain of laughter. "She could have bought a $1000 painting by the time you see her again."

"Not Gladdy," he said. "Not her." She wouldn't dare, not without asking him. She knew they couldn't afford it, even if she did see something she liked.

Though he wouldn't be surprised to hear Kit O'Donnell paid a fortune for something to hang in that boathouse shack she lived in. She'd done sillier things.

And wore clothes that no-one but a husband should see. Carl didn't know where to look; the front was split open right down to her damn belly button. And slit up her skirt so all the world could see leg right to the hip.

He rooted around in his pocket and brought out his handkerchief, already damp, and passed it over his forehead, around his neck. The heat in this place, the heat could be over 100. And all these people were breathing up the air.

"What do you think?" he said, and nodded his head at all of it. She was a teacher and perhaps she could tell him what it was all about.

"Think?" she said, and raised an eyebrow as if it had never occurred to her.

"Of this, of him, of his stuff."

"Oh," she said, "that." And looked blank as if already she'd forgotten the question, or him, or both. Then, suddenly, when he'd nearly walked away, she came to life again, sucked in air.

"He puts on a good show," she said. Dismissing it, perhaps. She wasn't impressed.

"He got a crowd."

"He got a crowd. But the paintings disappear in a place like this. Side by side, hanging, you suddenly realize what they are—products. In his studio, one at a time, they can suck you in. When I sat for him he let me see just one painting a day, no more. Each was like a fist in the stomach."

"You sat? He painted you?"

She chewed on her bottom lip and studied him. One finger slid down her naked front. "A whole series," she said. "Nearly every evening for two or three months."

"I didn't know, I never seen any of them. What part of the hall are they in?"

She put fingers, hot as electric bars, on his hand. "I've got to teach in this town," she said, and slid her eyes to one side. "I asked him not to display, not this time, not here."

The old goat. Had this little girl on up there in his studio every night for three months. Didn't do nudies, eh? Didn't *show* nudies maybe but he did them all right. Like every other damn one of them so-called artists.

"No. 97," he said. "I think that's the number they said.

"For?"

"For the painting of this here mug. I may as well take a quick look at it before I get out of here."

She turned and led him through the crowd. They threaded their way past moving couples, between talking clusters, around knots of gawkers. She led him right down to the far end of the hall where the crowd was thinner, all the way down to the corner. Then she stood back for him to see, as if she were the painter.

What he saw first was Gladdy, standing alone, staring at the picture, her head cocked to one side. Her long dress stretched tight across her rear end. Her tight shoes apart for balance.

Then the painting.

"Well shoot," he said. Because there must be a mistake. They were at the wrong one.

No. 97, though. And he couldn't deny the tuft of hair at his throat. Or the white stretch of forehead high into his thinning hair.

"Well shoot," he said.

Because it wasn't him at all. Not his face. Not any face he'd ever seen in a mirror. It was as if his face had been wiped partially off, then painted back on again just slightly altered so that it was someone else's, a stranger's. If he met this fellow on the street he'd pass him by without even thinking there was a resemblance.

"That looks more like old Wainamoinen himself than me."

Gladdy turned and just barely smiled and said, "Oh it's you all right."

And Kit said, "It's not bad at all. Though a bit unusual for him."

The face which was not quite his face filled up most of the left half of the canvas. Looking out, as if the frame was actually a window through which he could watch with cold marble eyes all these people watching him. On the right, behind him, was the new foundation of a house being built on a rise of stones and weeds, and on the foundation, a few perfect pink studs stood up as if they had grown there, or been nailed down at random, though at the top of one there was a small branch of leaves still alive, curving upward: an impossibility. The sky behind was the worst; it came right down to the foundation, right down to the man's shoulders; and it was white, nearly white. As if it were both nothing at all and a terrible threat. Because there were faint shadows in it, like pale grey smoke, that might have been anything, as if you were meant to peel it away to reveal what was hidden within.

A man with that sky at his back would be cold all the time.

"Son of a bitch," Carl Roote muttered. And hoped no-one else had seen him there. To guess.

"$800," Gladdy cried, consulting the price list taped to the wall. Her finger moved across the paper. "No. 97. *The Builder*. $800. That's what she told me."

Kit O'Donnell smiled. "He promised you immortality," she said. "Maybe what he meant was you'll be paying for it forever."

"I ain't buying it," Carl growled.

"But who?" Gladdy said, and sidled up to the picture as if she owned it already and he was threatening to give it away.

"Let some other stupid bastard pay to hang it on his wall," he said. "Right now I'm getting out of here."

In the basement suite of the artist's house Sparkle danced. Her body twisted and shook, jolted, twisted and shook, in the middle of the living-room floor. Hands flashed. Her hair whip-cracked in light.

The radio was turned up full volume, the house was solid sound. There wasn't another soul here but her—all the old creeps had gone. She was alone.

Twisted and shook, jolted, twisted and shook. Outside, the bay faded, the town translated itself into a band of yellow lights.

Hear it, hear it, she cried. Hear it, hear it.

Gladdy Roote could've bawled. Right into her pink lady. Men! She gritted her teeth to keep from speaking her thoughts.

They expected at least a clap of thunder. Or slashes of light. They thought that scales should fall.

Though she felt warm at the gaining of friendship. Kit O'Donnell had come in here with them, and argued with her against Carl's preference for the beer parlour, had ordered a pink lady too.

A corner table. Gladdy sat so that she could see, through the glass and across the foyer, the edges of movement in the wide doorway to the ballroom. And just by turning her head she could see the white stucco front of the Blessed Sleep Funeral Home through a window on the outside wall. It was a place you could sit all evening and never feel left out.

"I heard the brother agreed not to do anything to it until the three days were over," she said. "To the body."

Kit ran a finger around a stain on the arborite table. "Is that legal?"

"I don't know, but I guess for a relative you can bend things a little."

Gladdy looked across the table at her own closest relative. But Carl, scowling, hunched over his glass of beer as if he wanted to wrap his own shoulders around it, the only thing he intended to acknowledge in this world.

"You can't deny he's attracted attention," Kit said. "For a painter."

"I suppose the papers are here."

"The locals," she said. "I don't imagine the Vancouver papers would send across a real art critic."

"It's possible," Gladdy said, and sipped. "Anything is possible."

The girl's great dark eyes travelled all around the inside of the lounge. "Yes, I imagine," she said. And laced her long hands together on the table, scarlet nails like petals of blood on the white. What Gladdy would give for nails again!

Others had come in from the art show, talking excitedly at their tables. The jangle of bracelets, the baritone laughter. Gladdy could not want to be anywhere else, she was alive here. If only they wouldn't notice the misery implied by Carl's posture.

"I should've come alone," she said. "To spare Carl."

Who grunted.

"Oh no!" the girl cried. "I'm always surprised to see one of you without the other. It never seems right. You two are one of those couples it seems impossible to imagine apart."

Carl lifted his face to look at her out of one eye. As if Kit had just now landed there, from Mars. Then he looked down and drank the beer, his third. Gladdy felt cold breezes at her neck.

"Oh, we know what it's like to be apart," she said. "We haven't always been together."

"It still wouldn't seem right."

"The operation," Gladdy said. And rejoiced at the sudden rigidity of Carl's shoulders, of his huge arms.

"The operation?"

"All that time, while I was laid out flat in the hospital he cooked like a woman, looked after Sparkle, kept house as clean as if I'd been there. All that time, we were apart."

She cocked her head.

"Mind you, he used to come up to the hospital every evening and just sit there, staring at me. And cry when he had to go."

Carl put his big hands around her wrist. "All right, Gladdy."

"But I told him it was good practice for him. I told him

116

'What if?' you know, 'What if?' but he said he'd never get used to it in a hundred years. He said he'd rather they cut off his privates than take me from him."

The hand jerked away. She'd gone too far. Even the little teacher was blushing.

"Well excuse me," Gladdy said, and stood up. "While I visit the powder room."

And Kit too, was standing. "I'll go with you." And followed. You might have thought the two of them were running away from that brooding hulk. She saw the bloodshot eyes slide up at her from under his brows. He was sulking; he would sulk for a good while yet.

Kit went for a mirror, to fuss with her hair, and Gladdy slipped into a cubicle, shut the door. "Did you ever imagine," she said, "the network of pipes there has to be under this town just to keep places like this ready for these little emergencies?"

Kit admitted that the thought had never occurred to her. She said if you started to think about all the complicated workings behind every simple part of your life you'd never be able to move.

"Ha!" said Gladdy Roote, and lowered her behind onto the black cold horseshoe seat.

Then added, "Did you see old Carl's face when he took a look at that picture? I thought he was going to drop dead out of shock, right there."

Kit's voice was high, more English than she'd thought. "He must have expected a photograph. He must have thought Eli's brushes were meant to do what a camera does."

"800 bucks for that!"

"Well he'd probably lower the price a little if you were the ones to buy it."

"He could drop it all the way down to a dime and I know Carl wouldn't have that thing hanging in the house.

Though he may be willing to pay for the right to chop it up in pieces."

And then she noticed.

A seam in her dress had opened up for a foot or so down the front. The stitching was right out, a long white thread. If she'd pulled it the gash would lengthen all the way up to her waist.

Jesus Christ. She rummaged in her purse. For pins. For anything. You couldn't count on anything going right, it seemed. She turned over everything, all the combs and peppermints and bits of paper. She began taking everything out, one piece at a time, and laying it on the floor, but soon there was nothing left but fluff and grit at the bottom.

"What's going on in there?" Kit called. And laughed. "What are you doing?"

Throwing everything back into the purse. God damn this thing. How many people had noticed anyway? It was what happened when you had to make your own clothes, with an old machine. She'd never do it again, she'd steal first. The thought of those babes out there, noticing, laughing. She could spit.

And did. Straight into the toilet just as she pressed the lever.

"My bloody seam. Look," she said to Kit when she came out. And waited while the girl went through her own purse and came up with two straight pins, enough to get her through the evening.

"You're a doll, thanks," she said. And touched the girl, lightly, on the bare arm.

"Not at all," she laughed, and checked herself in the mirror, made a face. "You can't let a thing like that spoil your night."

"You can't let anything spoil anything," Gladdy said. "Not when you expect it will end. Some day."

Kit O'Donnell coughed, turning away. Tucking things back into her purse. Snapping the catch.

"Well," Gladdy said, and straightened everything, lifted her chin. "Let's go see if my old man's still pouting."

He was. Beautifully. His face like a brooding cloud hung over those beers. His red eyes shifted to watch them approach, then scowled again at the sudden appearance of someone else.

Eli Wainamoinen. Walking like a young man, at his age. Flushed.

Gladdy and Kit slid into their seats just as he arrived, his fingers playing with his own enormous ring. He tilted, nearly bowed; Gladdy could've snorted easily. Who was he suddenly, the Finnish ambassador?

"Carl?" he said.

Carl sat back, looked up. He showed his snoose-stained teeth.

"Carl, a gentleman has just approached me, from Victoria. He says he wants to buy *The Builder* but I told him not until I've spoken with my friend Carl Roote. In case."

"In case what?" Carl said.

"In case you want to buy it, stupid," Gladdy said. And nudged him with her elbow. "In case you don't want that someone else to own your picture."

"He likes it very much," the old man said. "He's a wealthy man, owns a huge house-building business. He told me he wants to hang the painting in his office!"

"His office!" Gladdy cried. Because who ever heard of putting out that kind of money for an office picture? Carl's office when he had one had two calendars for decoration, one of them several years old, both of them with pictures of hunters knee-deep in field-grass pointing shotguns at flying ducks.

"Well bully for him," Carl said. And drained his glass.

"I wouldn't say yes to him until I'd spoken to you. In case."

Carl looked at Gladdy, held his eyes steady on hers. "Well Mr. Wainamoinen," he said, "you let that fellow have the bastard painting. It hasn't got nothing to do with me. It don't even look like me. And all that other shit you promised me. . ."

"Promised you?"

"All that crap. You laid out a hell of a lot of paint onto that canvas, Mr. Wainamoinen, but you never laid out no heaven. A camera could of done better."

"Jesus," Gladdy said. And shook her head. And waited.

Wainamoinen sat. He felt, suddenly, that his bones could easily have been 200 years old. Carl Roote and Gladdy and Kit O'Donnell looked at him as if they expected him to shatter, fall apart, disintegrate.

You offered what you had to give and they did one of two things every time: didn't recognize what it was or rejected it without even looking.

"When you moved into my house I'm afraid I thought of you as my children," he said. To Gladdy. You couldn't expect Carl to look up. "I'd just lost my son and then you came along. I would've done anything. I told Sylvi she'd have to watch me, I might do anything I was such a fool. Just watch, I told her, they'll be up to complain about that tree, they'll be hollering they can't see the view just the same as Robert did, can't see anything but all those trunks. And I was willing, it didn't matter to me, we see right over the top. I would've chopped it down if you asked."

Carl looked up. His face glistened with sweat. "All we wanted was a place to live."

"Of course," Wainamoinen said. "And that is the point. I'm always trying to give people more than they want. It is a fault of many old men."

"I wouldn't've called it a fault exactly," Gladdy said.

"Oh but it is. When it intrudes. When it disappoints."

"We all disappoint," said the girl, and looked at the floor. "No-one knows that better than a teacher."

"And have our faults," Gladdy said.

Though from the look on Carl's face you wouldn't think he was ready to agree.

"Still," Wainamoinen said. "There is more in that painting. If you had only looked at it. I've given you. . . given you, what you want, what you said."

But there was nothing in those faces to show they were listening. Or cared.

Then Gladdy Roote brought her hand up to her throat. "Look!" she said, and pointed out the window. "David Payne. He's coming out of that place, out of that funeral place."

Carl didn't hear the first time she said it. He was thinking of the three beers and the painting. Wishing he could be at home tipping back a bottle from his own fridge. With Gladdy in the other chair drinking beer too with him, instead of that pale stinking gin in its silly glass.

Then: "David."

David Payne, where? Where the hell did she see him?

He twisted, nearly swept the table with his elbow, strained his neck to see. Out in the almost-dark the bastard was coming down those steps, watching for traffic, running fingers of one hand back and forth across the back of his neck. He looked like he'd seen a goblin, or a ghost.

All at once, something inside Carl leapt.

"What?" Kit said. "What is it?"

"Look out, you'll knock the bloody table over!" Gladdy threw her weight to counter-balance his threat.

"Aw," he said.

He would've pushed them all.

But they jumped back, let him free. Gladdy screeching: "Watch out what you're doing, can't you. Look what you spilled on my dress!"

Wainamoinen gestured, his hands helpless, his stiff face crumbling.

"Excuse me," he said, as if he'd been the one to knock the table. "Pardon me."

He stood in front of Kit. "Carl, Carl."

Carl only grunted. And pushed past, bumping one shoulder against the wall. "Shit."

If this was it! If this was the goddamn thing, wouldn't they just look. These other bastards with their show, all of them, wouldn't they just sit up at the difference? What would a bunch of paintings add up to then?

In his hurry to get out into the foyer he nearly fell over someone. But he ducked aside and went across the red startling carpet (people turning, he couldn't say who, and saying "What's wrong?" and "Who's that?") and managed to straighten himself and slow down a little by the time he got to the oak door.

The smell of gasoline exhaust. And pulp mill. The shock of the light flashing violet neon from the sign: HOTEL ARBUTUS HOTEL. Down on the sidewalk he waited for a truck and camper to pass. "Yaw!" he yelled at the driver, a bulge-eyed American staring at him, slowing down. But the truck stopped right in front of him and the driver stuck his head out the window: "We just got off the ferry. Where's your liquor store?" Carl yelled, "Yaw" again and gestured for him to move on out of the way. "Bugger off, mister, go on out of here."

David Payne when the truck had moved was holding onto the lamp post at the edge of the sidewalk, hunched over and staring down at the street as if he expected to be sick.

"What happened?" Carl said. "What happened there?" His chest hummed with the possibilities, his head throbbed.

But David Payne's face was yellow, his eyes ringed with dark smudges. "Hunh?" he said. And shook his head. His hand on the post was fat and short, like mottled raw sausage.

So Carl went right on past. Though the sight of any funeral home was enough to make his stomach knot, it was plain he was going to have to go inside this one.

He had to see whatever it was that had yellowed David's face, sent him outside. He had to face that woman and her damn coffin.

Or whatever.

Behind him, the others had come out onto the street too. He could hear. Let them come, let them follow. Let them have something to talk about tomorrow.

He couldn't help noticing someone had done a hurry-up job on the concrete steps, lousy trowel work, with ridges and hollows. It was his unthinking habit whenever he entered a new building to estimate the size of rooms by counting plywood panels or ceiling beams or imaginary paces down the length of floor, and to pass judgment on the quality of the finishing work (mitre joints of casings told the story, and cupboard doors). But when he left the foyer and walked across the second room of the Blessed Sleep Funeral Home, where a person would normally expect to find a body laid out, there was no time or inclination for estimating, there was only a vague impression of polished coffins sitting around on chrome legs. And in a third room beyond, there was only Anna Payne laid out on a small bed in the very centre, blankets pulled up to her chin like someone sleeping. And Carrie Payne, looking at him down the length of it.

"Carl," she said. You'd think it was the name of a little boy who had run to her for comfort.

He'd never before seen such a face. Swollen. Those two eyes which must've gradually been getting bigger every minute since Monday morning were looking at him now as if he should have been able to walk right on inside and disappear.

"Oh God, Carl, I think she moved."

His throat clamped. "What? Now? Just now?" Because if it was, he was running.

She shook her head. "Earlier. I was sure of it. I could've sworn she moved, just the smallest bit."

She offered it like a shy gift but he could've puked. He couldn't even let himself look down at the girl, whose head was just inches below Carrie Payne's chin. Her hands were down somewhere underneath as if she were ready to haul that body right up into a sitting position for him to face.

"Goddammit, Carrie," he said. "Are you sure?"

"Of course she's not sure."

It was David's voice, behind, in the doorway. "She only thinks she saw."

"I was sure of it, David." Now she was someone begging for favours. "I was sure I saw her move."

Carl turned. If David Payne hadn't been in the doorway he might have run. But the little man stood there as if he expected to fall, and lifted up his face just far enough to look out from under those eyebrows. "Don't lie, Carrie," he said. "It's only because you were so sure. It's only because you expected."

Outside, a car braked, suddenly. The tires screeched, it seemed, down the full length of the block.

Wainamoinen on the steps of the Arbutus Hotel watched the car skid to a stop. Then he followed the others across the street as far as the door to the funeral home. Something heavy sat on his chest, however, and he turned to start back toward the hotel, moving slowly through the neon violet like a swimmer.

Gladdy said "Ah!" and bit her lip.

Everyone was going up those steps after Carl and David. Pushing against shoulders.

She put her hand on the pale flesh of Kit's arm. "You don't suppose?" she said. And swallowed.

"Don't be silly."

The girl had the kindness to soften the words with the quick touch of fingers.

Still, a person couldn't just turn her back and pretend. "Maybe Carl needs me in there."

The girl, though, was not convinced. Or raised an eyebrow at least to question. So Gladdy added: "Who knows what the bugger might do," and stepped forward to follow the others.

If there had been a way of avoiding this she would take it, provided no-one noticed. If she could have refused to put one foot inside that place, avoid getting the chilled skin called up by velvet and candles and polished wood. But she couldn't leave Carl like that, when his mind was thrashing about, when he might not be able to stomach it. He didn't know that you couldn't conquer it by fearing it, any more than you could by daring it or by tempting it or by accepting it.

"Well, if it happens," she reminded herself, "You won't see my ass for dust."

She was, too, spared the unpleasantness of witnessing. Whatever had been going on had reached an end. Someone rushed out past her, hand on his mouth, muttering "Jesus Christ," and nearly fell over his own feet to avoid bumping

125

her. And a woman, following, touched Gladdy's arm. "There's no point going in," she said. "Leave the poor things alone."

Clutching her purse she stepped into the room, smelled the thick heavy scent of flowers and furniture polish, felt the breathing, the shifting of feet. Was there a decent way to enter such a place? All eyes seemed happy to turn her way, to avoid whatever else there was.

But looking straight at things was one demand Gladdy Roote had always made of herself. Directly ahead was Carrie Payne, standing over a bed as if it was something she needed to defend. She glanced up at Gladdy out of one eye from under a wing of hair which had fallen.

But it was David, not Gladdy, who attacked. "Can't you see what fools we've become? Look, they're crowding in to stare at us."

At the same time, he put a hand on her arm as if to give her comfort too, or maybe just to keep from falling over. Carrie only strengthened her grip on whatever she had ahold of at the top end of the bed. A dark-suited man who must have been the brother hovering about, fluttering, looked ready to scream at the chaos which had broken out in his premises. He looked like a man who was considering a blow to the side of his sister's head to bring her to her senses.

David: "Think of the number of people who die every day in this world. Out of all that tell me how you dare to expect one girl to be chosen for this special privilege? Do you think we are so different?"

And Carrie: "How do you know how He works? You don't know Him. I saw her move."

Gladdy's knees gave under her, she could've dropped. Something gurgled in her stomach.

David was trying to pull her hands away, trying to loosen

126

their grip on the bed. "It's only because you refuse to admit," he said.

And Carl too, now, was getting in on the act. He placed a big hand on David's shoulder. "Leave her alone. She's got a right to expect."

But David flung him off.

Gladdy said, "Carl," and bit her lip. He didn't hear.

"She's got a right," he said. "You can't blame a person for being on the side of life. There's enough of the bastards already to take the other side."

Gladdy thought it was a laugh that lifted in her chest but it was a hiccough instead. She couldn't be sure how many heard and anyway it didn't matter because now David was trying to push Carl toward the door. "Go on away," he said. "Leave us alone." And to them all: "Leave us alone can't you? Leave us alone."

But Carl wasn't giving in. Not yet. "That picture too," he said. "That bastard picture turned out to be nothing."

David Payne might not have heard. Gladdy didn't know whether to drag Carl out or leave by herself and let him find his own way out of the mess he was making. Now that he was getting louder.

"You'd think he'd painted the all-time masterpiece the way he carried on, the way he talked. But it was nothing. Nothing at all." He clasped a hand around the thin arm of David Payne. "You would of expected it to be something more than that."

"No," David said. "Go away, Carl. Leave us be. Go on back where you were."

So he pulled on the arm, nearly yanked the little man off balance. Shouting now. "But there's got to be something!" His eyes, bloodshot, toured the room until they found Gladdy. She could feel their two glances lock like the snap of a screen door closing. "Because if I lose her! Because if I goddamn lose her!"

Then he bolted.

She could've cried, the way he looked at her. As if somebody had come up behind and hit him on the head with a great wooden mallet. Seeing something he hadn't seen before, or hadn't been there.

She snapped eyes at Carrie, at David, and said, "Well, if anybody's risen this day it wasn't in the flesh," before hurrying out to the foyer. She could almost have added, "Nor was it one of the Paynes, either," if there wasn't this something in her throat. She thought of rummaging in her purse, in the junk again, for a hanky. . . anything. But she found, quite surprisingly, that there was no need after all for the hanky or for anything else to stall her. She snapped the purse closed and hurried outside.

The street, a little darker now, was nearly deserted. Only a few stragglers on the other side, around the hotel doorway. Carl was seated on the top step of the Funeral Home with his back against the door frame, watching his own hands out of eyes that had shrunk down to the dull stone hardness of late-season blackberries. Like a man, perhaps, who sits amongst the leaves and sawdust in the open bed of a pickup truck, just waiting to be taken somewhere.

"When I saw it wasn't going to happen I was glad," he said. "I would've been just as scared of it as you. Scareder."

"Still, it's only natural, I guess. To want some kind of sign."

"Hell Gladdy." His hand clamped around one of her ankles. "That's what I mean." He ran the hand up her leg. "Any bugger who's saddled with an old rip like you for a wife's got no business looking for signs. It's them other people that have to make them up. The ones that don't trust something." The ones that don't trust something." The hand moved away then, fanned lightly across the concrete

128

step. "Lookit this mess, Gladdy. Too damned rushed to do a decent trowel job of it. They couldn't wait for it to set right."

She moved the toe of her shoe over the offending step. As if she could feel, through sole, the imperfections his hand could detect almost without touch. "Let's go home."

He pulled his hand back in, started to rise, and then slumped again. "Aw Gladdy, don't go, not yet. Sit here for a while. Just till I catch my breath."

"Sit on cement?" she said. But sat, all the same, and smiled. The bloody dress had already fallen apart—what more damage could she do it?

She looked out across the street to where the HOTEL AR-BUTUS HOTEL sign splashed light down the front of the building and out over the roofs of cars. Someone inside the ballroom laughed. Gladdy Roote in that moment swelled, throbbed, with the rich blood of her possibilities.

Prelude to a Parking Lot

Elizabeth Spencer

Who are we? Look and see.

Look out from your upstairs window at night, across the cinder alley that leads off the shady street that slants down from Twenty-first Avenue that crosses the west end of Nashville. See us in the lighted bay window below.

We are sitting at the dining-room table—round, old-fashioned, with a white cloth—eating strawberries with cream and sugar. Or blackberries maybe. The milk turns purple. Have some more. Not but one or two left. Have you heard and did you know? There's Brother, big and growing, and Uncle, way too fat. There's Mother and my first cousin Janey and me. Uncle and his daughter Janey own the house. Mother and Brother and I moved in after Daddy died. It was too big for two and we had nowhere to go. We hated to stay on in the country. Mother said she could do a lot of things but not farm. She didn't have the slightest notion of how to do it. It's funny because she heard Daddy talking about it for fifteen years, but when Brother accused her of never having heard a word, she finally admitted that was true. "I just never thought I'd need to know," was what she said.

For a long time after I graduated from high school and got a job I was happy to think I was making a living and pulling my own weight. This gave me real satisfaction. My small room, no bigger than a good-sized bathroom, became my domain; my importance filled it neatly, to the crevices. A new kind of lipstick bore itself upright on my dresser with a glistening air of something picked out and knowing it; it could companion me for quite some time. New shoes gave my legs what they wanted to feel about themselves, and I had different feelings for every dress and blouse. I ironed a lot and washed a lot, did my own hair and for imagination drew on a stack of books from the library which I was always changing for new ones.

Looking down on us, at the round table, though you can't hear what we say, you may see us laugh. Very few people find each other funny in a good way. We do. We are funny to one another.

All except Janey. But that's another story.

Uncle Jess is the one we all get exasperated with, in an affectionate way. He won't take himself seriously enough to get ahead. He has retreated into high blood pressure. But really he lacks confidence; he moves timidly out in the world.

What Uncle Jess likes best is to do something we all will laugh at him about. This way he gets to be himself; it pleases him to be remarked on. But he knows you can't fake it, or you'll just be boring. If you put the radio on and lie out on the little back porch in hot weather on the cot and go to sleep and not hear a word, then you have got to really go to sleep, not just pretend. Then when we call him to supper and he comes in,

"What was on the news?" we say. "How are they getting on in Korea?"

"Hard to tell when you don't know none of them names," he says.

"Hard to tell when you're asleep," Brother says.

"Naw, that ain't it. What I need is a map. Look like the war's go' be over 'fore I get it."

"Good Christmas present," Mother says. "A map of Korea."

Janey doesn't say anything. She knows we're having fun but she won't join in. She's got on black lipstick. She has long thin nails, like splinters. The trouble with her not saying anything, she makes everybody nervous. And she knows it. She does it for meanness.

Look fast if you want to see us. We seem to be eternal, even though common as weeds—eating and laughing and talking, five in all; but one by one we won't be there. I'm the youngest, and change for me has set in already. It started that very day.

At the firm that afternoon they had sent me upstairs to an executive meeting to take down everything everybody said. It was a day of new shoes (pumps) and good legs, one of my days, hair burnished and lipstick neat. I turned out a cracking good job. It was more than a job; it was also a performance. If they had cast Lana Turner for the role back when she was nineteen or so, she couldn't have been more convincing. I had always been quick in shorthand, like some women can sit in the movies and knit without missing either a stitch or a scene. There had been a shake-up in the law firm because one partner's nit-wit brother, who had been holding an office, had at last seen the light and got the message and decided he had better devote himself to raising Tennessee walking horses. Reorganization was now indicated. The law firm was always calibrating itself more and more closely into the needs of certain large businesses it represented. And there were tie-ins with real-estate ventures and with powers in the legislature—a top-level meeting removed others from the scene in the wake of the dumb brother. Now they were rechanneling their streams and rerouting their traffic. I sat and did pothooks with my back straight and my legs crossed, feeling pretty.

"Did you get that, Miss Stacey?"

"Yes, sir, shall I read it back?"

"Just that last part, if you don't mind."

And I did.

Somebody eventually sent out for sandwiches and coffee. It was while we were eating that one or two of the men began to ask me questions—where I was from, how long with the firm, where did I live now, what about my family?

"They'll be stealing you next," said Mr. Eric Porter, my boss and not on the stationery yet.

"Not a bad idea," said Mr. Reginald Burns, silver-haired, looking at my knee.

There was general laughter. The feeling was good.

It was late when we broke up and Mr. Eric Porter offered me a lift home. I felt he'd seen me for the first time when Mr. Reginald Burns had said what he did while looking at my knee. Mr. Eric Porter had got nervous with all that shuffling around of big Nashville names, both within the firm and the fabric of society. The business world made him nervous. When he just dealt person-to-person he was calm and able. But mention the world-in-general and something made him swallow, tightened the corners of his mouth, glazed his eyes, reminded him that his office was at the far end of the corridor and had no carpet as yet (though one was ordered). That particular night when what rattled him had been constantly under discussion all day long, he felt the need to be steadied by some outer source of strength. He stopped in front of a house across and up the street from ours for a minute and put his hand on my knee, right where Mr. Reginald Burns' eye had rested.

I felt myself wake up all over, as much or more than if

he'd kissed me, and knew that I personally was never going to feel the same about Mr. Eric Porter.

After a time, he removed his hand, plastered a casual kiss on my forhead and drove on to my front door. "Good night, Miss Stacey," he said as I got out.

After sitting all of a spring afternoon and into the night with my heels deep in rich carpeting, and the smell of oiled mahogony and the discreet cluck of brass-fitted doors and drawers opening and closing, the way our house looked seemed out of the question for a fine attractive bright modern girl like myself to put up with. Mr. Eric Porter had a wife, though the office gossip was that he wasn't happy with her, and she wanted him to do better, and it certainly sounded like all of this and more when they spoke on the telephone. But still, he had her, so I decided I wouldn't even think about him.

But then he asked me for a beer and a hamburger one night when I worked overtime, and then we detoured once on the way home out to Percy Warner Park, which turned out to be a 25-mile ride with him telling me his troubles and some kissing thrown in, and I knew I'd better quit that job the next morning. But I didn't.

Percy Warner is a big, beautiful, accessible park and was where I fell in love with Mr. Eric Porter, who wished he was married to me instead of Mrs. Porter but whose career could not, at this point, stand up under a divorce, Mrs. Porter being from a prominent family.

The first year I did nothing but worry, decide and undecide, but the second year I settled down to seeing him without worrying much. The word, I later learned, is accommodation.

The third year Janey got mad at me over a bridge party I had promised to help her with but had only remembered during a movie when it was half over. She then said she had known all along about Mr. Eric Porter. She told Mother out and out, though Mother in some sort of way, not admitting it, had known it too, and she said further that she had a way of getting the word to Mrs. Eric Porter, who was dumb enough to believe her husband was late with important clients once a week, and had joined a volunteer civic group but had to quit, being pregnant.

"Yes, pregnant!" Janey repeated, brows rushing together, sticking her face close out to mine over a bowl of chicken salad.

I hadn't known and couldn't believe it. I couldn't stand to think about it.

Next day at work I got sick and asked to go home early.

"What's the matter?" he said. We'd gotten long ago into an act in the office, blank and professional as strangers.

"Nothing," I said.

A pause.

"Well, it's none of my business," he said.

Another pause.

Then, as we were alone with the door closed, he said: "Tell me anyway."

"Is your wife expecting?"

"Well—I meant to tell you, but I—It doesn't make any difference—"

"Difference! It makes me sick."

He had the nerve to grin. "It made her sick at first, but now it doesn't."

"I'm quitting this job."

"We can't talk now. We'll talk later."

"You've as good as put me in a bucket and run me down a well. You haul me up once a week and look at me, then you put me down the well again."

"I do more than look at you," he pointed out, no quarrel with the rest. "Oh, come on, now," he said, and caught my arm.

The door was opening. Somebody had knocked but we hadn't heard, over in the corner by the files, quarreling in whispers that went up like steam on a hot stove.

I went out in a streak and left him to make up whatever tale he wanted to tell.

The next day I took the day off. They could fire me or not. I took the bus out of town, out toward the Hermitage. The Hermitage is a big antebellum home built by President Andrew Jackson, "Old Hickory."

I had to get away because, at the house, Mother was wandering around debating what to say to me. I didn't go to the mansion but stopped in a town nearby, had a coke in the drugstore, and got to talking to an old woman who was sitting on a front porch. She had asked me to close her gate when I went by, and instead of closing myself out, I went in. I sat down on the edge of her porch. She did not find this remarkable, but said she saw I was worried. I said that I had meant to get married and that now I wouldn't be able to, as this man was not only married already but was also expecting a family. I shouldn't have told her all this. She would know somebody and tell. She said I was young and pretty yet, and would get over it. "Go find yourself somebody else," was her advice.

I wondered then what old women sat and thought about and how they could stand it, being old. No new pumps would ever make their legs look good again, no man would ever sigh or catch his breath when he looked at them. This one sat with her knees apart, cotton skirts to her ankles, hands laced together, lying in her lap. She looked happy, she was rocking and smiling now. She had some memories, I guessed, but I wondered if memories, even happy ones, are good enough to live on.

"Don't tell anybody," I said.

"Don't see nobody to tell," she said, which is not a good answer. It meant that if she did see somebody to tell, she would.

I got the bus and went home.

It was fall and getting chilly. There was a smell in the air, a dusty smell, that comes, in our part of the world, from the leaves when they turn colour and crumble in the dry air.

The next day, Mr. Reginald Burns called me in and said he had heard about another office which wanted a good secretary rather badly. He said there would be more chance of advancement in this new firm. I nodded and said okay. I agreed with everything he said to keep from crying. All the time I was gathering up my things my eyes kept blurring and running with tears. Mr. Eric Porter wasn't there that day. I thought I'd never see him again. For one minute I considered leaving him a note on a leaf of shorthand paper, but decided that was not the way to say anything.

I did not like the new office I went to as it was a long way by bus in a rather run-down part, over toward Centennial Park where they have a replica of the Parthenon and a lake, too. But now that I had a Past and thought I was making a New Start, I made the Best of It and I was on the way to Better Things. After a week, Mr. Eric Porter called up and wanted to see me one more time to talk things over, so we started going out to Percy Warner Park again. There didn't seem to be any way to stop because the shade of too many hackberry trees, black by moonlight, the sound of too many little streams, the inside of the big family car, and each familiar touch and word—all belonged to us alone, in the sense we knew them. He said he just couldn't understand it, the way we were, but he thought we were always going to be that way, let's face it. He said his wife had heard some gossip at long last but knew I was out of the way and gone God knew where.

"I told her you'd moved to Atlanta," he said.

"That sounds like the Penitentiary," I said.

He said she had always believed he had really had night work and that he had seen me only a few times. He said she didn't know my name and didn't want to know it. He also said she had almost lost her baby. (He said her, not their.)

The next week we were debating with a good deal of cold-blooded happiness just how long after a baby arrived its father could conveniently ask for a divorce. He didn't care if it hurt his career or not, for without me life was not life at all.

Along about then he got a promotion and his wife came into some money. They got a much bigger house, further out in Belle Meade. He had to play at the good life, he said, even if it was only a game. He would always be responsible to me. I was the heart of his heart, and the good life was not only a play, but it was the game—did I understand that? —the game that everybody played. You couldn't jump off the world. Anywhere he went he would only be a small-time lawyer, competent, not brilliant. Here in Nashville, all the right names and things collected around him, only here could he play the game. What else could he do?

But I knew the baby had come, and all he was saying was words.

I moved out for a time. I got a room in a section which had a lot of Jews in it, up above Centennial Park. I never knew that part existed. I never knew so many Jews existed, not in Nashville. I thought they were alive and interesting. They were mysterious. The men, though often ugly (sometimes not), looked individually sexy, each in his chosen way. In my world men wear careful masks. Yet I couldn't tell just why these people were doing anything. For instance, when I saw them walking in the streets I wouldn't know for sure where they were going, or why.

For a month in that strange part, among those people, I thought I too, along with Mrs. Eric Porter, was going to have a baby. I felt sick a good bit and I thought this was why.

I went to see a doctor about an abortion—it was a woman doctor who didn't practice openly. She was in her late forties, I guess, and looked like she must have cried quite a bit herself, from time to time. She was going to do the rabbit test, so I left.

On the way back on the bus, I decided I wouldn't go through with any abortion, I would have that baby instead. This was my Great Decision. I felt very good about it— good for ever, a pure sort of goodness. More than that, I felt alive and felt the life in everything we passed. Every driveway and lawnmower and grass blade and doormat had its secret life; and each was shouting silently, giving and giving it. More than that first touch on my knee and all that followed, it wakened me, but in a new way. I would go to another city and have the baby and work for it and that would be my life. I would say its father got killed in the war. I would tell it this.

I stopped back by the old house to see Mother. She was there but not Janey, thank God. Uncle Jess had a job, for a change. Mother had kept up with me on the telephone and I had all the news, but now she told me again as if she hadn't. In a blur of joy, I sat and rocked in time with the world, which was harmonizing like a Grand Ole Opry tune.

That night in my lonely upstairs room in the Jewish section, I found that the child would not be born after all, if it ever had existed. I never knew. I called the woman doctor the next morning to tell her. She said, "That often happens," and click went the phone; so out of my life went the baby, a leaf blown off the steps.

It was the idea that stuck with me: my exaltation, the

world's secret life, and the thought of holding on.

My only question: Would I have had the guts to go through with it? My answer: Yes.

For: The high-water mark in my own little history had been struck and my soul created. I wanted to leave Eric now. That white, shivering bus ride when I came out from Ward-Belmont Way into Twenty-first Avenue and decided not to throw it out with the garbage, this had changed me. Changing me, it had changed the way I felt about Eric.

We argued.

"You wouldn't have had the nerve," he said; and I said: "Just because you haven't got any nerve is no sign I haven't."

You can't get over speeches like that. You think you can, but they are always there, waiting for you to come back to them, purring like two cats, keeping the chairs warm for you.

In those days I used to go on Saturdays that were sunny and warm and sit in Centennial Park, sometimes on the grass. A picture of myself seems to form in my mind, a girl with long dark hair hanging down (I put it up on working days) and legs folded to one side, one arm straight, the wrist pressed into the grass, the other hand lying in my lap. I'm not sure of so much accuracy here, and maybe it only happened once or twice. Maybe other times I sat on a bench, for the ground in autumn and spring is usually cold. Still, the picture endures.

One day I returned home and took my old room back. Nobody had moved into it, though Brother was thinking of fixing it up for a TV viewing room, but Uncle Jess was saying it was too close in there for everybody to get in at once so leave the set in the living-room where it belonged. I ended the argument when I came back.

I was happy that first night and cried no more.

In my narrow room, comb, brush, mirror, powder and lipsticks lined up on the dresser, I was at peace. I felt timeless. This could go on forever, I thought. Why not? I thought.

There is a woman working at the bank on the corner near Peabody College, and she has been there since I can remember. She will stay there till she retires, I guess. Then she will live alone, see the friends she's always had, go to church, read books; one day she will fall ill, go in a nursing home or to a hospital; one day she will die. What's wrong with this? What's to stop life from happening in this peaceful way? Is it so bad? If it is not so bad, why does it make me want to scream with anguish and fear? If I want to scream with anguish and fear, why don't I do it? Instead I come home from work, watch TV, help get supper, help wash up, shampoo my hair, do my nails, read, fall asleep. The one thing I try not to do is quarrel with Janey. Some days I hate her, some days I merely despise her.

Janey is getting married. Her fiancé is younger than she and is from some little hole in the road, he says Yes, ma'am and No, ma'am to Mother, but he is an intern at the hospital, from somewhere he got the money to finish med school and being a doctor will put him up in the world. Janey knows this. She also knows why he likes her. So do I. He has plump hands and close-together eyes. Janey doesn't love him, she has never shown love for anybody that I know of, but she is ready to get married. Mother says:

"Janey wants you for her only attendant. We're going to have it at home. She'll wear white. We've all decided to chip in for her. Will you?"

I can't afford it. But it was something to deprive myself to contribute to, just to get her out of the house. I knew I had to anyway. Mother with her little farm income and the house to run always made me feel sorry. She was pretty and ought to have had better. She would put out all she could out of gratitude to Uncle Jess. Brother had got married secretly. (He walked out one day and came back married. He introduced his wife all around, then they left. He came for his stuff later.) We had rented his room for a time to a nice quiet girl.

Twice she went out with some friends and stayed later than we locked up. She had forgotten her key both times, and the second time she swore not to do it again, never, never.

"It's not that important," Mother said. "Don't worry about it."

I thought she was afraid of us, but maybe she was afraid of the world.

"I ought to talk to her," Mother said, "but I don't know what to say."

Then she forgot her key the third time.

It was a freezing cold night. She sat out in the car (she had a little car) alone for three hours, nearly freezing to death, shivering and quaking. I guess she would have stayed there all night but Mother woke up and looked out the window. She put on her flannel robe and went down to let her in.

"Don't worry about it," she said. "It's not important."

The next day when the girl came home from work she went to her room without saying anything. We were all around the dining-room table (except Brother, who had got married). There was a long silence, then we heard her door close and presently she appeared in the dining-room door. She was thin already, but now she looked drawn, and all I thought was that she was coming down with a cold from sitting out in freezing weather so long and wanted an aspirin. But she just stood there stiff as a cold poker till we all looked up, then she said in a quavering voice:

"I don't understand you. You don't understand me. I

don't like any of you. I think you're horrible. You're awful people. It's why I keep forgetting my key. I really don't want to remember it, that's why. It smells funny here. I have to leave."

We got shocked by this, as nobody could think of any way to dispute her. Maybe we were horrible, maybe we didn't understand her, maybe we did (though not aware of it) smell funny, maybe she did keep forgetting her key because she didn't really want to remember it.

Then, for the first time I really missed Brother. I understood him then, his worth. If he had been there he would have had something to say back. I could just hear him.

For instance: "You come on in here and have some of this chocolate cake." (Making her feel better.)

Or, "What a coincidence! We think you smell funny, too." (Making us feel better.)

Or, "Come on, now. Which one of your boyfriends stole that key?" (Making her and us both feel better for more complicated reasons; among them: she didn't have any boyfriends but would have been flattered to have him pretend to think so.)

Brother could have made all the difference. As it was, it seemed to me later that everything that was changing picked up a vastly accelerated rate after that girl stood there accusing us and we let her get away with it. She was what Mr. Eric Porter, who had majored in literature before he went to law school, called a Greek character, a messenger the gods know about, but you don't. Not till they give you the message. Then you know.

After Janey married and left, Uncle Jess and I used to sit out on the back porch after I came home from work and talk about things. This was the first time we ever did get to talk. Before, he was just somebody there. Like I was born with

143

fingers and toes, so I was born with Uncle Jess. But one day he started talking to me. Maybe he had got tired of reading the paper and listening to the news. He couldn't work (it was understood) because of high blood pressure. In reality, he could never keep a job, but we didn't mention it.

He said, first of all, that he knew I had never liked Janey. Then he said that Janey was not really his own daughter. Her mother, Aunt Edna, now dead, had been playing around with somebody else the summer before Janey was born. Janey knew about herself. This is what had kept Janey from ever having much feeling, she had this about herself and what her mother had done in her mind all the time. One night Uncle Jess had got drunk, "when you were just a little ole thing," he said.

"How little an ole thing?" I asked.

"In yo' *crib*!" cried Uncle Jess.

Well, we'd never had a crib there, but there was an old white-painted child's bed in the attic with a rose appliquéd onto the footboard, so I let it pass.

"I kept saying to Janey, 'Come here to me, I'll make you mine,' I said it over and over. Being drunk, I couldn't quit once I started. You know what your Momma thought? Thought I was trying things on that child."

He was awe-struck at the thought and we both got embarrassed. I fell to remembering the day he had found Brother and Janey out in the garage and had chased Brother around the yard with a bed slat. We did seem like an odd family. But for pointing it out, that girl had dealt us the *coup de grâce*.

Uncle Jess was a big rounded-out man. He was so perfectly rounded-out that you couldn't tell how big he was at first, then it would dawn on you gradually and rather splendidly, like a sunrise. He was like a girlfriend of mine at the office who had taken a European tour said about some cupids in the Vatican at Rome, they just looked like little bitty things, then you would get close and find they were three times as big as you with wrists you couldn't get both hands around. Uncle Jess had a face as big as a close-up on a movie screen; great flat pads for feet—he wore black leather laced-up shoes—and big soft puffy hands. His eyes looked pressed into his face like they'd chosen him a pair too small and then it was too late to swap them. You would never know what colour they were, they were too deep in there to see. I can see how Mother might have been horrified with a little child asleep in her white bed, a three- or four-year-old girl in the house and that big hulk of a brother-in-law, wild drunk, going on about, "Come here, I'll make you mine." But just the same I wanted to giggle. I saw it the way Mr. Eric Porter might have. He had a good sense of humour.

But I didn't laugh.

"I built a boat," said Uncle Jess, on another afternoon entirely. "You remember that boat, Sister. Out in the back yard."

I did remember the boat, though my thoughts in those days were all for Mr. Eric Porter.

Also, I forgot to say, Mother had bought the house from Uncle Jess. She had come into a little money when Grand-daddy died, out in the country, and she and Uncle Jess had gone through arrangements so complicated it's a wonder to me they ever did get done with them. They filled up three dime-store ruled tablets just with their figuring and calculations. The upshot was that Mother got the house, Uncle Jess invested the money she paid for it and what with his unemployment cheque could afford to give Mother money for his room and board. He was also going to do the yard and handy work, painting and all that, just like always. There was a big scramble over who was going to pay for upkeep, tools, paint, grass seed, what to do if the garage fell down or the tree died or lightning struck us, no end of considerations. He couldn't have got by with any borrowing of so much as a splinter from our premises to start building on a boat, so he must have scavenged wood from here and there and bought nails, bolts and hardware out of his pocket money once he quit drinking. Whatever he did, Mother felt she couldn't challenge him about it as he had to have something new now he'd given up liquor and she didn't want to start him up again.

At first we didn't even know what it was. It was like one of those puzzles in the paper that you take a pencil to work out. You go from 1 to 2 to 3 and you zig and zag and by the time you go to 59 or 103 you've got a picture of a boat. We suspected that it was a house and that he was going to move out into it only it was too little for him as yet to get more than one foot and leg into it. Then the spar went up and we recognized the curvature of the hull.

"I aim to live on it," said Uncle Jess.

"Out in the back yard?" Mother inquired.

"Don't be a goose," said Uncle Jess. "On the Cumberland River."

We were all at the table (before anybody married) in real hot weather drinking iced tea and eating icebox lemon pie.

"There's people all over the world lives on houseboats. There's just a world of people does it. I don't mean to forget all y'awl. Y'awl can come spend the weekends. Maybe not everybody at once."

"I wouldn't be caught dead in that thing," said Janey.

But Mother thanked him politely. Part of it was, she would have been relieved to have him elsewhere. Brother was a great big boy and felt confined with all of us in one house.

Mother told me years afterward that she thought Brother

146

and Janey had "something to do" with one another. "She was no blood kin," Mother said, "and Brother knew it, some way or other."

"*She* knew it," I said. "Uncle Jess told me she did."

"I don't think it was true," Mother said. "I think she was Jess and Edna's child. Edna was scared to death of Jess, just like I was, when he was drinking, only more than me."

There comes a time when you know you're not going to marry anybody in a certain town. It was just that everybody in Nashville had known about Mr. Eric Porter and me, or so I thought for a long time. Then one day I knew and not only knew but told myself right out that nobody in Nashville was going to marry me whether there had been any gossip about Mr. Eric Porter and me or not. I got some proposals but not from anybody I liked. So I joined an agency and, in time, got an offer in Atlanta. A month later I got engaged. It happened sooner than I thought.

I asked Mother, "What makes you think that Janey and Brother had something to do with each other?"

"Well," said Mother, not surprised that five years had elapsed since she mentioned it, "I went up in the attic one warm spring day because I missed them. I'd sent one of them to the grocery and the other to the cleaners and I thought it was time at least one of them was back, if not both. Then it just came to me that's where they were and I'd better get up there quick. I climbed the back stair and opened the attic door and—well, there they were."

"You're kidding!"

"It hadn't gone all that far. He had her black hair wadded in his fist and her head pulled back, bending over her. She jumped up and back like turning loose of a spring. She just plain glared at me, and Brother didn't feel like saying much of anything. I just said, 'I thought you all were up

147

here.' And left. I didn't mention it to Jess. How many other times? I kept thinking, lying awake at night. Maybe that was all, though. How do you do."

She said the latter because my fiancé had just walked into the restaurant in Atlanta where he was taking us to lunch. They were meeting for the first time. They said later they were just crazy about each other.

Mother wouldn't move to Atlanta, though we asked her to. It turned out that all along she'd known how to type, so she freshened up on it and put her card up at Scarritt, Peabody and Vanderbilt. No end of things came pouring in. Theses, term papers, dissertations, even poetry. She had to put a limit on what she could accept. I sent money home and so did Brother.

It was only Janey wouldn't send any money home. She never came there except about twice a year as a sort of duty. She wore very good-looking clothes, more "outfits" than what you would call ordinary clothes, and she had lovely rings, a gold chain like I always wanted (I had a fake one), three wristwatches—sport, regular and evening—and alligator bags. Mother never asked her for money. I guess Uncle Jess never asked her either. I guess too it was just as well she didn't come too often. She had a lot of people to talk about up in Jackson, Tennessee—people who belonged to the horse-show crowd and the country club, were golfers too, and went to the West Indies in the winter. Every time she left, Uncle Jess would be rather afflicted in some way, Mother couldn't say just how, though she understood it. He would mope around, she said. We agreed he was trying to shake her off.

Mother was down in Atlanta to visit us when she said this. She comes once or twice a year. That night we got a telephone call from the Nashville City Hospital. Uncle Jess was in it. We left right away.

148

What had happened was strange, but then he was always a strange man. Left all alone, he had gone down to the Cumberland River and tried to drown himself. It was down where he'd hoped to be, I guess, at least had dreamed of, had spoken of, living in his houseboat. And maybe he hadn't tried to drown himself but had just wanted to investigate the depth of the water, the lay of the banks, what it would be like. If so, however, 11.30 PM was an odd time to do it.

Some Negroes pulled him out. They'd heard something out in the night splashing and floundering around like a hippopotamus, they said. We had compared Uncle Jess to a lot of things—an elephant, a balloon man that you go to the gas station to have blown up where it says Free Air and then you can't push him over, a baby cupid 43 times normal size in the Vatican in Rome, etc.—but had never thought of a hippopotamus. But then we'd never seen him sloshing around in the Cumberland River.

"We had us a time gittin' him outa there," the Negroes told us, when we went down and found them. We wanted to give them something, but they wouldn't accept. "He a big man," was all they kept saying, "He sho' a big man," they said.

At the hospital Uncle Jess loked pale. His hair had got greyer and sparser without our noticing the change. It stuck up against the white pilows. He was talking prety wild.

"Looks like I can't step out the door something don't happen," Mother said. "Jess," she said, "I ain't ever going to leave you again." (Mother doesn't say ain't but Uncle Jess does; she said it for him.)

He kept on talking wild, but finally we got what he was trying to tell. He had just been up to the corner for a hamburger at the Krystal Grill—by that he meant at least three of them; it took a lot to fill him up—when he came back to the house and knew it wasn't empty. He thought it was

Mother back but he walked into the dining-room and there at the table sat Aunt Edna. She was waiting. He'd said she was dead so often he had almost believed it was true. But she had never died. She'd left him, that's all. And left her daughter, too, who was not even his daughter.

He said: "Edna, what on earth are you doing here?" And she said: "I've come back to you, Jess. To you and Janey." He said: "But Janey's got married, she's not even here." She said: "All right, then I've come back just to you." And he said: "But why'd you want to do that?" And she said: "Because I love you, Jess."

He felt dizzy and went to the kitchen to get some ice-water. He reached to draw the jug out of the refrigerator, and that was the last he remembered.

He didn't remember about the Cumberland River or the Negroes and didn't know anything about how the bottles got into the remains of the old boat hull we still had stored out in the garage. We had put it in there after Brother left; he was the only one of us that ever had a car.

It is the thought of Uncle Jess wandering around alone and drunk from right after lunch till 11.30 PM that I can't get out of my head. It's a home movie that I can't shut off; I can't find the stop button.

The places he went. . . the streets he wandered in and out or. . . the people he passed. . . . The ones who didn't know him. . . the ones who did. . . the dogs he stopped to pet. . . the things he fell over. . . .

It fell my lot to call up Janey in Jackson, Tennessee. She was "out," her maid told me; but finally she was "in."

"Edna's dead as anything," Mother said. "She's buried up in Winchester Cemetery. I read it in the paper. It's true she did go off with somebody else, but in the beginning she did love Jess. She had this disappointment because he never could make do in a job. *He* thought it was his funny looks, his size and all. It was just a sort of permanent misunderstanding. But she's as dead as anybody can be."

But Uncle Jess couldn't get her out of his head. She was part of his reality, or rather his life-long parade of realities, one after another, the street-length of them, each turning our corner, approaching in full detail, regalia and flourish, then passing on in time, gone in one way but in another never gone, as each had become its own history. Like Janey and all of us moving in on him and the boat and the war news and the house sale to Mother and the jobs and Janey's marriage (he rented a swallow-tail coat to give her away), Aunt Edna's return was with him forever: it sat in his head, the table and her sitting at it just as he'd seen it when he came in from the Krystal Grill. He has it with him now in the nursing home. That's the only place it is, or can be.

For: the house, the one we used to live in, the one I've talked about all this time, the one that had the table you could look down on and see us all together at, talking and laughing and eating blackberries which make your tongue turn purple—it's sold and torn down. You couldn't even look down on it any more because the house next door where you were has met the same fate. It and ours and two more. They're all a parking lot now. All cemented over, smooth and grey. After surgery comes the neat scar.

When in Nashville, I go to see Mother. She's moved into an apartment in that same neighbourhood. She couldn't give up her neighbourhood, she says. Then I go to visit Uncle Jess in the nursing home. His mind never came back right, after that day.

I say: "I believe you, Uncle Jess. She was there. And she did love you. That was true."

I can say that so it convinces and soothes him because of that baby I was going to keep. Not those I finally had, but the one that never was, and how I felt about it, that one day.

Perhaps the Church Building Itself

Kent Thompson

It is perhaps the church building itself that attracts me on these fine autumn afternoons. I tell myself I want merely to get out of the house for a bit, catch a breath of fresh air, escape from that soliloquy of questions and answers which Mrs. Harrison, my housekeeper, considers conversation. ("What are you going to do today?" "Nothing," I say. "Surely you're going to do something—do you want to talk?" "No," I say. "Not to you." She sniffs.) She is so easily offended. If I tell her that I am not interested in conversation, she says she is not holding a conversation, that she is merely making small-talk. The distinction she makes between the two remains mysterious to me. Nor can she understand in the least that I do not like small-talk. To her, small-talk is a good thing: always has been; always will be. So I escape.

Yet, though I tell myself it is an escape, it is not. I leave the house—sometimes make a show of going elsewhere; sometimes, in fact, make a trip around the block for no other reason than that I must delude myself—but I always know where I am going. I am going to the church.

It is at the end of Milton Street, which is named after my grandfather on my mother's side. Indeed, I was told often enough as a child how all this was once my Grandfather

Frank Milton's farm, and, when I was a child, I remember trying to imagine cows grazing on the knoll where the church is—where the church was, even then. The passage of years has been good for it, I believe, because the horse-chestnut tree in the lawn in front of the church, just near the notice-board, has grown to an adult height. And the brick of the church has weathered into something dusky, subdued, a dark shadow with some deep red in it, a texture and colour that seem to indicate a stability through the seasons and a particular affinity for autumn. The ivy which now adorns the front of the church has softened its lines—and that, too, is a good thing.

When it was built—I was just a child, of course—it seemed to me to be very raw—indeed, quite uncomfortable. I attended it in company with my parents, and, to me, the rough slashes of raw dirt about the flat stone step at the doorway and the chafing of the starched white collar at my neck were much the same thing. The harshness of the situation, the rawness of the building—both hurt me, then.

Now, however, the building pleases me. The town did not grow any farther in this direction. When what was once my grandfather's farm had become the preferred residential section of the town, the town seemed to have satisfied itself. Perhaps even money can be satisfied. I don't know. But I know that now, when one stands on the lawn in front of the church, yes, under the horse-chesnut, one can see the cows of Evans' Dairy grazing peacefully a couple of hundred yards away. They stand—caramel and white—and shuffle ponderously among the fallen golden leaves. Evans once worked for my grandfather, I believe. I remember him as a short man with extraordinarily long arms—and a small shiny head. He wore a red-and-black checked flannel shirt. His arms strained at the cuffs.

Perhaps I am trying to recapture my youth when I go to

the church on these fine afternoons, although why I should want to do so puzzles me, because I always found the church an uncomfortable place, though tall and sweet. My father was a deacon, and while he and his friends were busy gathering the collection and attending to the duties of the church, I had to sit uncomfortably beside my mother and try to think of something to do with my hands—something acceptable—while my stomach growled and I longed for dinner. I would have liked to have drawn pictures while I sat there, I believe, although that would have been completely unacceptable.

But I know what I did do.

I sat there and dreamed a future to myself—and became properly terrified when, as my youthful years went on, those dreams were increasingly full of women who progressively wore less and less clothing until one day I was sitting there staring into the middle distance at an imaginary nude woman when the minister's face came suddenly into focus right through her belly. I have forgotten his name. He was staring directly at me and saying something quite innocuous—something like "And so I say unto you that the meek shall inherit the earth"—but the phrase struck me with a guilt quite as piercingly as if it had been a direct accusation. Perhaps, I thought, he could read minds—and it was very nervously indeed that I asked my parents at dinner afterwards if, in their opinion, he possessed that ability.

Father was brief: "He doesn't even know his own," he said—and poured gravy over the mashed potatoes.

But Father's attitude changed over the years as well. When I was a middle-aged man it struck me as quite amusing that Father should worry himself sick trying to decide what verse should go under the stained-glass window he was preparing to offer to the church. It was no small matter to him *then,* I assure you. He wrestled with the decision—asked his old friends over to the house to solicit their advice, asked even me, and bothered the minister until the fellow had come to believe he was destined for sainthood or perhaps martyrdom—simply because of my father's demands. when the time came—when the time was past due, in fact—and one of his fellow deacons said to him that they had to have his decision that weekend or else they would have to turn to somebody else (the church had become fashionable, you see, and there was a sudden rush to replace the sober, plain-glass windows with deeply, brightly coloured figures, and there was no shortage of donors), Father threw up his long-veined hands in angry desperation, went into an old man's sulk, and informed my mother that she must make the choice. She did so, and I believe she did it at random. She simply flipped open the New Testament and dropped her finger on a verse.

She often did that. I saw her do it countless times when I was a boy. In fact she came to her Bible several times a day.

"Why are you doing that?" I asked her.

"I want to *know.*" she replied mysteriously.

"Know what?" I said.

"Never mind," she said. "It's my business."

This did not prevent her, of course, from moving her finger about on the thin page to find a verse she "liked." And I think this was certainly the case when she came to choose a verse for the stained-glass window. She chose: "Whosoever shall seek to save his life shall lose it; and whosoever shall lose his life shall preserve it" (Luke 17:33).

And that is what I find when I go to the church on these fine afternoons. I have a key to the building, of course, and I simply let myself in and stand there, in the quiet of the church, then walk soft-footed down the aisle, up to the pulpit, and stand behind it, looking out at the empty, polished pews and the sweet sunlight streaming in through the stained-glass window donated by my father.

There is a fern in a pot-stand by the side door; it has turned yellow from too much sun, and droops.

Sometimes Rev. Williams is in the building and, hearing me, comes in to give me a glance and a quick wave before retreating to his study.

He leaves me alone; I leave him alone. I do not wish to cause him trouble. I am too old to cause anyone trouble, would not, I think, if I could. I will allow him to have his ideas if he will allow me to have mine.

And he does indeed have ideas. He is a young chap, and I am taken aback a bit by the way he runs true to type. Surely, I think, given the infinite variety of humanity, all young clergymen should not look the same. Yet he looks like his predecessor, who looked like his, and so on and so forth, right back to the first nameless one I remember. Their eyes are small and grey, and all, all of them have rosy cheeks as if they had shaved with a razor which was much too dull. All of them wear their hair parted on the left side, and cut rather short. All of them lean forward to grasp the sides of the pulpit when they are coming to the message of the sermon, and all allow their voices to fall nearly to a whisper when they do so.

One learned very quickly to catch the signals. Everyone did so—even my mother. When the sermon fell to its whisper, I could see her tense herself in her seat and lean forward, and *almost* reach for the hymnal—because she was so sure we were just at the point where the Minister would say, "And now let us stand for the closing hymn and remain standing for the benediction." The tone of his voice was that everything was now put well to rights, and therefore everyone in the church recognized the completion of the service. Everyone knew. You could hear, in fact, the slight creakings of the pews when the moment of the whisper came.

So, if Rev. Williams thinks that it is merely my age that sometimes makes me call him by the name of one of his predecessors, he is only partly right. My confusion is due also to the fact that he—and all of them—run so completely to type.

And thus, when he gives me the little glance of recognition and the brief wave of greeting and leaves me alone, closing the door that leads to his study behind him, I sometimes wonder: who has been there and where has he gone? I look at the dust floating in the sunlight, and at the empty pews. I try to puzzle things out—and am grateful to him for allowing me the privacy of my contemplation.

Then I walk home, where I am sure to find a plate of cookies and a glass of milk left for me by Mrs. Harrison, who has by this time gone home. I sit in my study and drink the milk and eat the cookies, rising some two hours later to go to the kitchen to see what she has left in the oven for my supper. And the fact is that if I have had a thought—a single thought of any kind at all—during those two hours, I do not know of it.

On Wednesday evenings we meet for discussions. This is a practice started by Rev. Williams' predecessor-but-one and continued because there are some of us who enjoy it so much that we refuse to let it die. The discussions mean a great deal to me, and to Mrs. Turner, to Harry Tilden and Les Howe, to Mary Wright and her mother. I am sure that Rev. Williams thinks we attend simply because most of us are old and have nothing better to do, are lonely, in fact—but this is not entirely true. There is a searching which goes on in old people's minds—at least until their minds break down—which cannot be imagined by anyone who is not old. We want to *know* something—and are willing to learn almost *anything* as a means of reaching for the answer to the great question.

That question, of course, is: What next?

My father died without finding the answer for himself, and it was a sad departure of a kind that I am trying to avoid. The last two years of his life were spent in a wheel-chair, and he rolled from room to room on the ground floor of the house, looking, looking—always looking intently, curiously, as if he expected it would be there, somehow, in a book, in an object, in a person. Perhaps he expected a vision; perhaps he thought he had earned the right to have a vision after all those years of tithing, after all his years of service as a deacon. But his mind was going and it was painful to watch him as he struggled for a word which would not come, and then, at the end, struggled for even the thought which could not be summoned any longer. He looked like a puzzled monkey. My mother broke down and wept.

And she, too, wanted an answer, and by this time her Bible was limp from being flipped open, its thin, red-and-black pages smudged from her fingers as she came quickly from the kitchen or the garden to search in the random chances for an answer. And it was clear that she was not finding it. Some of the pages of the Bible were torn—for she was thrusting her finger down now more in accusation than in question.

None of this meant much to me, of course. I thought: they are old and ill and are going to die soon. They are confused. I have a household to support and look after and am doing my Christian duty as I see it simply in attending them and making their last years as pleasant as I can.

I did not see their desperate searching, of course. I would

not have recognized it if I had.

But I think I see it in our discussion group, although it is obviously true that not one of us has the courage to ask the forbidden question directly. Or else we have such good manners that we cannot.

Can any of us—can Mary Wright, for example—ask so blunt a question of young Rev. Williams? Mary Wright is the youngest of us, at 71. What if she said, leaning forward as she does when she becomes agitated, her lower lip quivering with anxiety: "What next? That's what I want to know —what next?"

I can imagine that the poor fellow would stumble for a moment before replying, almost gasp for breath, perhaps, or reach impossibly into the empty air, before giving us any one of the answers that he might think suitable: "We can only pray," perhaps, or: "That—I'm afraid—is quite beyond me." And he might well laugh at himself, or blush.

And we in our group might then sit staring at him angrily, all of us wondering just what all this has been for if you can't get a straight answer to a straight question.

And perhaps it is simply because he is afraid of our harsh question that Rev. Williams—who is a shy man, in fact— has begun to turn the "discussion group" into a *class*, and a class, moreover, which is as much concerned with current events as it is with religion. It was not long ago, in fact, that he suggested that we turn our attention to "the tragedy of Northern Ireland." He looked at me and asked me if I would like to do "a bit of research on the subject."

And I, like a fool—or a good-mannered old gentleman —agreed. What else do I have to do with my time?

But, like a lazy schoolboy, I put off doing it. The week went by, somehow, and I did nothing about it. Where the time went I do not know. What I did with my time remains a mystery to me. One day for me is very much like another unless something special is to take place, and that happens rarely enough. Generally I sit in my study and observe the weather. The weather is my chief hobby—although I take no notes, keep no records, as some do. Yet I knew one morning that it was Wednesday, and the thought struck me that morning, as I read the latest death figures from that troubled island in my *Telegraph-Journal*, that the day was upon me, that I had a promise to keep, and that I had done nothing about it.

As it happened, it was raining that day—one of those cold grey autumn rains which indicate the end of autumn. I put on my rubbers and took my umbrella and stepped out on the verandah, thinking that by tomorrow the trees would be black and barren, and that shortly, there would be frozen puddles on the sidewalks.

I made my way carefully to the public library, thinking, as I did so, that very few people realize how slippery wet leaves can be. I took that as a good omen: that I had found a small thought to entertain Miss Wright and the others, and I planned to say, "Perhaps I should make note of a discovery which I made today. Wet leaves are very slippery." The *tininess* of the thought amused me.

But I could easily imagine what Rev. Williams' reaction might be. How banal, he would think, and his face would have that surprised, stunned look that young people have when confronted by what they take to be the obvious or the trivial. What a ridiculous thing to say, he would think, looking away. Surely our Mr. Wilson is beginning to sink into senility, he would think, and it's only the matter of a brief time before we shall be putting him into Bethel home, and after that, a grave. Yes.

Indeed, I can easily imagine Rev. Williams sifting through

his mind very quickly for the proper verses to read at my grave.

Well, that's as it may be. I am sure he thinks like that—and equally sure he does not know that all of us realize he thinks like that. For my statement, banal as it might be, would have the effect of invoking little smiles around our group. We would savour its tininess as one might savour a grain of salt. Understand me: we, as a group, have almost nothing in common except our advancing years. But we enjoy that bond. Miss Wright might well have smiled and told me that she had noticed the same thing. Les Howe—whose face has gone dark as a rotten walnut due to his heart condition—would have nodded. Only that: the nod. But we would all, I think, have leaned forward to one another. "Where two or three are gathered together." Yea, we are the church of the aged.

The rain was falling quite heavily by the time I reached the library—it had settled in for the day—and as I stepped inside, shook out my umbrella and placed it in the make-shift rack by the radiator there in the foyer, I took cognizance of all the familiar smells of the place. The moisture from my umbrella invigorated the dirt in the bottom of the boot-rack where the ferule of my umbrella was pointed: and it invoked a smell of manure. Someone had been in from the farm—last winter, probably—and the smell had lain there dormant, waiting for me. I seemed to recall following my grandfather out to the barn of Evans' Dairy—we had gone to visit his former employee, just to see how he was getting on—and I was stepping carefully at first to avoid the muck. Then, realizing that I could not avoid it, I began stomping happily in it, well realizing that my grandfather would protect me from my mother. The result was as I predicted. My shiny black shoes were soon fertile with cow manure, my mother wept when she saw me, and grandfather handled the matter by saying roughly that she "should let the boy be." Everything was as it should have been, then.

And when I shook out my coat, I caught the familiar odour of wet wool. How good it smelled! I believe I was smiling as I stepped through the doors into the library itself—and I had reason to smile: my nose was in fine fettle that day. Ah, lyric nose. Lyric, lyric nose.

And that, in turn, gave me a feeling of sprightly confidence. Things were going well, I thought, and I nodded to Mrs. Warner—who was working behind the check-out desk—and murmured that I sometimes liked a good rain. She, quite taken aback by the comment and obviously forgetting the season, said something about it being good for the crops.

The seasons mean nothing to her. Well, that is understandable: she is not yet an old bird.

And then I caught a glimpse of a woman disappearing into the stacks and asked Mrs. Warner who that lady might be.

"Who?" she said.

"That woman who just went back there."

"That's Mrs. Hilton," she said. "Walter Hilton's wife. You know her. She's been working here for over a year now."

Of course. But what excited me about her had nothing to do with who she was, although of course I should have recognized her—*would* have recognized her if I had met her face-on.

I went directly to the reading room where the magazines are shelved—the current issues on a rack by the window and the recent back-issues stacked on shelves along the inside wall. I had no intention of doing any serious research on the subject of Northern Ireland. Rev. Williams was easily satisfied; too easily satisfied, in my opinion, and the others in the group were quite willing to accept anything one told them quite benignly. I intended simply to look through the more recent issues of *Time* magazine and gradually acquire a looking-backwards knowledge of the chief events in Northern Ireland's recent history. Surely, I thought, I would come upon one of those little articles so favoured by *Time* —a black-bordered, boxed article that summarized the tragic history of the place. That would be quite enough. Most of us would be eager to get to the hot chocolate and doughnuts provided by Rev. Williams' youngish wife anyway. It was the conversation we were after. No—not the conversation, but the quiet being-together.

And I suppose I was thinking of Rev. Williams' youngish wife and Mrs. Hilton, whom I had seen when I entered the library, even as I took the year's stack of *Time* magazines off the shelf and placed them on the round oak reading table. Their covers were a shuffle of pictures. I sat down before them and found myself in a muse.

Mrs. Hilton reminded me of someone: she was wearing a tailored tan suit of some soft material—and brown high-heeled shoes. That was it: the shoes had thrown my glance upward to the calves of her legs. They were strong, attractive. Women's stockings, I remembered, used to have seams up the back, and women used to worry a great deal about whether they were straight or not.

And that, in turn, reminded me of the woman I was searching for in my memory. It took some time before she arrived in my consciousness. I must have thought about twenty different women, rejecting them one by one, before she appeared. And this is the strange thing: not *one* of those women was my wife, Elizabeth, to whom I was married for 35 years before she died fifteen years ago.

When she died, I was then recently retired and planning to undertake some sort of local scholarly activity. I thought

163

I could write a history of the county, and I remember quite well abandoning the entire project simply because Les Howe (still a pink-faced if white-haired banker, then) said to me: "A good job for your retirement."

"Oh?" I said.

"You and Mrs. Wright," he grinned. He was, in fact, referring to Mary Wright's mother, who is now 87.

But it was the word "retirement" that offended me, I believe. Instead of working with Mary Wright's mother, therefore, I began to nag the town council to do something about the recreation facilities in the community. And that's why the tennis courts are named after me. That—and the fact that I donated half the cost of them.

But the woman of whom Mrs. Hilton had reminded me surprised me when she appeared. It was not someone I had known at all well, but was, in fact, a young woman—a girl, really—who had been employed in our office for perhaps a month or two back when Jimmy Porter was first made a partner. I believe his wife objected to the hiring of her, and now that I recall it, it was he who engaged her. How strange that I should think of her.

But I know exactly how I remember her. It was late one afternoon and I believe everyone else had left the office—so it was probably a Friday. I was working rather later than usual, because, I am sure, I had put off doing tasks I should have done earlier. I never enjoyed the practice of law. Father was a lawyer, and therefore I became one. It was easy enough in those days (before law school was necessary), and indeed, Father let me know more than once just how lucky I was to be following in his footsteps: "There's a good living just waiting for you," he said, "and you'll find that's the next best thing to a large inheritance." And, as to the inheritance, he let me know that he had no intention of dying unil a very ripe old age, and that he would probably spend most of his savings. This turned out to be true. He was retired for almost 30 years before he died, and his last illness used up most of his savings, going through interest and capital at a pace analogous to that of the disease which was destroying him. He was right.

But the girl was somehow still in the office, and I do not believe she knew I was there at all. There were no lights on —either in the outer office or the inner one. And yes, that was it: she must have been preparing to leave, and thought I had already gone—unless of course all this was done for my benefit! This has just occurred to me.

Yes, it is a very real possibility. Certainly. Yes. Yes. *She* could not have locked up the office because, as a relatively new employee, she could not have had a key. Miss Elsie therefore had left—and had told the girl, certainly, that I was still in the inner office and would lock up when I left.

I was probably staring out the window—I did a great deal of that, if the truth be known—as the evening fell. It was nearing dark. Yes, I remember that. It must have been autumn. Probably about the same time of year as now.

And the door to the inner office was not quite closed. There was just enough opening for me to see through into the outer office. And, turning from the window, I saw her: she had her foot up on the chair by her desk, and her skirt up around her waist: she was re-fastening the top of her silk stocking to her garter. The one leg was long and shapely, sleek in its silk with the seam straight. And the white thigh of the other leg flashed at me. Oh, it thrilled me!

How long I sat in front of the *Time* magazines I do not know, but I do know it was late. I came out of my reverie in a panic and began to glance through the magazines hurriedly, looking for the black-bordered box which I was now sure existed, and which, if I could only find it, would solve my dilemma. But if it existed, I could not find it. Again and again photographs of Ian Paisley leaped from the page shouting at me. A gross man, I thought. Gross. My hands fluttered ever more rapidly through the pages. I felt myself overwhelmed by the impossibility of the task. I began to ponder again, quite unwillingly, the reasons why I had never been appointed to the Bench.

Mrs. Warner, the librarian, was standing beside me. "Mr. Wilson," she said. "Is there anything I can do to help you?"

"What?" I said. "I do not understand."

"Are you looking for something in particular?"

"No," I said. "Just these years," I said, gesturing at the stack of *Time* magazines. "Just these years."

She nodded.

"Have I been asleep?"

"No," she smiled. "I don't believe so."

"What time is it?" I asked—for I was in such a panic that I dared not look at my own watch.

"It's nearly four."

"Nearly four!"

"Yes," she smiled.

What had happened to the day? It had gone—it was gone, gone, gone, and I had done nothing! I was horror-stricken.

"Please," I said. "I had better get home. Mrs. Harrison, my housekeeper, will be worried about me."

"She telephoned," said Mrs. Warner. "I told her you were here."

"I'll wager she was very put out."

"No," she replied. "I don't think so."

But everything then was such a rush. I was totally unprepared. The discussion group would be meeting in no more than three hours, and I had nothing to tell them.

166

I left the library in such a rush that I forgot my umbrella and made my way along the street and up the knoll toward the church. However would I explain this to Rev. Williams? What ever would he say?

Perhaps he might say: "I have never known Mr. Wilson to let us down before." He would be stern. Yes, I could imagine him being stern.

It was terrible—but there was no escaping it. I went on as rapidly as I could to the church and let myself in, relieved —in a way—to be safe and sound inside. Once inside, in fact, I felt *warm* and comfortable. The sweetness of the church rose, as if from a nest. And I meant to go see Rev. Williams—to throw myself on his mercy. Surely I intended that.

But I was led astray. I did not go to the study at all, but made my way, soft-footed down the centre aisle to the steps that led up to the pulpit. And there I lay down. I did not understand it. Too late, I thought. Too late.

I believe I was already weeping when I lay down—still in my coat—because my hat rolled off to one side ridiculously, and I paid no attention. It rolled down the three shallow steps on its brim, then fell over, its openness upward. I was weeping steadily by this time. The terror had taken complete possession of me.

It was this: I had the notion that somehow or other, when the mind "went," so too would all the involuntary muscles, and I could imagine myself as an absurd, dirty figure, lying there weeping while my shit and piss poured from me, filling up my clothes.

Indeed, I thought I was in exactly that state when Rev. Williams found me. He came up and knelt beside me, opened my coat and undid my waistcoat, and placed his ear to my heart.

"Rev. Williams!" I cried. "I'm so ashamed. I want to

die," I said.

"I understand," he said, and returned his head to my breast. "I understand. Lie still."

But he didn't—and I wept the more because I thought I sounded like some foolish old woman.

Cuixmala

Judith Penner

Alvaro says it means graveyard. Cuixmala. The rest don't
know what it means because the word is ancient Indian, not
Mexican. If they knew what it meant, says Alvaro, the
government would say the land, all of it, from the ocean far
up to the edge of the plantation, is theirs. An archaeological
site, theirs to dig up, his to mourn the loss. It belongs to him
even if he doesn't own it. He is the only one of all of them—
Antonio, Antonio's father John and Miguel, Antonio's
mother's father—who still lives here. The road was only
built two years ago. Before that, bush and semi-jungle for-
tressed the ranch so that anyone coming had to disembark
from boats or drop from planes. We came in by car. Alvaro
apologizes. He would like to take me up in the air but the
plane sits crippled in the yard. Yesterday the wing lay on
the ground for some repairs, he backed up the truck and
crushed it with the wheels. The plane is first of his many
children. Each piece dismantled and fitted back into the
whole with English words. English is a strain for him but he
knows every word of the plane's instruction book, had to
know, had to decipher each word so precisely that he never
forgot. Loose translation doesn't fix a plane.

He shows me the skull he dug up some years ago. His
first real find from the graveyard. It is smaller than I expect,

grey and dusty like the sand that held it—for how long: a thousand years? I ask. He doesn't know. It's a knowledge he forgoes in order to hold onto it. You and Mike, he says, I haven't shown the others.

When he came down to Miramar we were drinking Cuba Libres. Antonio and Cecilia had brought me back from the doctor's that day and the glass jar of deafness was still around my head. In the three days since my plane had landed in Manzanillo's field, my ears throbbing with pain from three descents along the way, I had been separated less by language than by muffled reception. Cecilia translated for the doctor, who stuck long pins into my nostrils and flushed my sinuses until I cried. Later, I lay on the couch at Señora Guzman's while they ate lunch and joked in family Spanish, inviting me to try the chili sauce, just a bit of eggs, Señora Guzman bringing me bread hot from her oven. The Spanish swirled around me like the dizziness, half heard, part understood, then spun up and down like cotton candy ravelling on and off the stick, drawing my dreams into the spin until I slept.

I wasn't supposed to drink the Cuba Libres. I wasn't supposed to drink anything too hot or too cold, especially alcohol or coffee, but there was nothing else to drink and by evening I felt somewhat better. When Alvaro arrived—it was his beachhouse we stayed in, Cecilia, Antonio, the two children and myself—we were celebrating my shaky return to conversation. Antonio spoke English as he spoke Spanish, with wide gestures and a loud voice swamped in laughter. You will love Alvaro, he said, everyone loves Alvaro. Alvaro will take care of you when we leave. Alvaro will take you to the ranch, the "rr" taking command of the word rrrrrranch. Alvaro will take you to the ranch. So Alvaro drove in on a fanfare of Antonio's words.

Alvaro Vasconcelos Juarez. He had been a beautiful man. He is still a beautiful man; once, more youthful. His stomach is larger now, though not offensive, his hair still thick and dark. On the wall that ran alongside the stairs to the second floor hung pictures of his airplane, his wife and his ten children.

We sat outside in a cocoon of dark air, watching the ocean, talking for an hour or so in English until Alvaro was tired of the struggle and Antonio could no longer hold in the run of words and shot into the race on home ground, his arms wild, his exclamations fierce, his words only on the slowdown round the curve decipherable to me. I didn't mind. Even their English seemed out of range. Luis smiled, talked softly, chuckled at Antonio's stories, egged him on affectionately.

On the drive to Cuixmala Alvaro sounded me out. He wasn't sure I'd like the ranch at all. Many hadn't. His wife lives in Colima now, with the children, though some of them have grown up and gone on their own. She endured the ranch as long as she could but finally moved back to town, to people, to shops which hold pretty dresses, to stores where furniture gleams with newness, where there is no need to sleep with the dogs. He built the beachhouse at Miramar for her sake but she still prefers the town. His children sometimes stay there, and Antonio and Cecilia on holidays. It isn't altogether a waste. And unlike the ranch, it does belong to him, on paper if not in spirit.

This morning I woke up to find him standing beside the bed, quietly calling my name. After Cecilia and Antonio left yesterday I found clean sheets and made up the big bed in one of the upstairs rooms. All the rooms but this one had at least two beds; most had four or five—for his children, I guess. The room downstairs where I'd been sleeping was dark, the sheets felt damp. Perhaps because I still wasn't feeling too well and because I was alone, surrounded by a beach, a flat long road, a language I didn't understand but would like to have heard now instead of my own thoughts, the upstairs room gave me comfort. The books in my bag—Pablo Neruda, D. H. Lawrence in Mexico, Henry Moore in Greece—spoke with distant words. I found a scrap of a gossip magazine and read about Mexican movie stars. Alvaro hadn't arrived when I fell asleep.

Waking up to see him there I thought: I want him in my bed, then covered my bare shoulders. He had breakfast waiting: eggs and instant coffee and some of the children's milk Cecilia had left in the fridge. In the downstairs bedroom I gathered up my things—toothbrush, underwear, a a jacket, a book I didn't think I'd read. I didn't pack my cotton skirt—Antonio had laughed when he'd seen it and said I wouldn't need to dress up here—or my yellow platform shoes. A pen. A notebook. A towel. My jeans weren't entirely comfortable. I could see in the mirror how round my stomach looked in them and tried to suck it in.

The hacienda is almost bare inside. The beachhouse was plain too but it had the plainness of new things barely tempered by belongings. Alvaro and Mike, his nephew and foreman, live alone in the hacienda, making do with a few dishes, a long table in the sunporch along the side, miscellaneous chairs, beds—there are too many of them here as well as at the beachhouse—and a smaller table in the centre room which supports a ham radio set. There are six rooms, including the bathroom, all of them large. But the house has grace —low, worn stone, wide porches, uneven tile floors. One hundred years ago Antonio's grandfather chose this hill to set it on, the only hill on the entire plantation from which everything can be seen.

I sit on the stone wall set against the porch and watch

hawks scrawling formations on the sky. Insects I have never seen before scratch hieroglyphs about my feet. Two kinds of butterflies, one yellow, one white, flit up and down the grass. I can see the ocean far over to my left, below me thick rows of trees bearing the fruit named—Alvaro has patiently made me repeat it until I say it right—*platino macho.* They look like large bananas and may be just that. Every time I forget the name I am embarrassed at the paucity of my Spanish vocabulary, at the fact that Alvaro, who speaks decent English learned on his own from an airplane manual, has to put up with me, who cannot remember the Mexican word for banana. There are orange groves too, tall bands of coconut trees—their tops like curls to run your hand through, wide clumps supporting pineapples. At the bottom of the hill that leads down from the house are squats of workers' houses, identical, shabby, grey as the sand. As plain as the house on the hill, but smaller. Each hut has its chili plant beside the door, its burial ground for corn.

It's pay day. Alvaro and Mike wave me down to the big tree where everyone gathers on Fridays to receive the wage prescribed by the government. 30 pesos a day, 50 pesos a day for those who drive the tractors and trucks. Manuel. . . Benito. . . Guillermo. . . Jose. . . they acknowledge my strange presence with shy smiles, brief chatter amongst themselves, jokes that bring gentle laughter. When everyone is paid, the flap on the back of the truck swung up and hitched, the cash box closed, we sit in the softening sun to drink tequila from the bottle Alvaro passes around, relaxed against the bole-like bench that holds the tree.

Everything on the ranch belongs with him. He names the trees for me, touches fruit, shows me where this new ditch will go, how guavas will be grown here where the land was barren before, and these strong trees, we'll leave them, they've grown here long enough to earn the right to stay, pleased it is all new to me, delighted that I love it. We drive in the truck for a while, over to Benito's hut at the edge of the mango grove, past herds of Brahmin cattle whose loose neck skin slaps against the long grass of a new grazing pasture, past a lake, past the songs and whistling tunes of men building a shed. When we walk he shows me the smaller, more intimate facets of the ranch. His pact with all these things is private, has nothing to do with profit, yield or documents of ownership. But he seems anxious to share it with me, as though his love for the place has been taken as much for granted by his friends and family as the jacarandas and poincianas whose vibrant colours no longer sting eyes that see too much of them. This is only a feeling I have; I don't know. There have been bits and pieces of information dropped in conversation: how his wife finally left, she'd had enough, how even Antonio, whose family owns the ranch, does not bother to visit, how visitors find the house too bare, the ranch too far from easy entertainments. And here I am, falling in love wtih everything he shows me but more and more confused when everything he shows me becomes a gift, a conjuring, out of green growth, red jewels for the lady.

When we reach the coconut grove he presents me with a coconut, but he has to make several tries to get it. Each time he jumps to knock it down his machete seems to slice the light that arrows through the treetops. On the third try he severs the coconut's hold, ducks before it hits him, catches it, and cuts the top off almost in one move. Only a slight faltering, the heaviness of his body meeting the ground, mars a once-unconscious motion. It is a courtly gesture I'm not sure how to accept. He wants me to like the coconut tree and the milk, but it's the first I've ever had straight from the tree and the milk tastes odd and not quite sweet. I tell myself it is only a holiday treat, no more. Canadian. Too young for him. My first time so close to the tropics and still half sealed to things.

We walked about a mile beyond the coconut grove into a low place closer to the ocean, where shrubs bend into a lagoon. A rowboat is hitched to one of the small trees. Alvaro unties it and I help him push it down into the water, then step in while he holds it. He takes his shoes off with one hand and rolls his trousers up to his knees, one hand still on the boat. Then he gives the boat a shove, it slides onto the water, and with a run, his stomach swaying slightly as he moves, he follows the boat, heaves himself up into it and grabs the oars. His legs are muddy and so are his trousers which have unrolled themselves and skimmed the surface of the water. He doesn't let me row. There is no sound except the slow slup slup of the oars making a mouth in the water—down the throat, up and over, slup. . . slup. . . slup, birds whistling short tunes across the air, the hum of nearby waves, and Alvaro breathing in gallant company with the rhythm of the oars. We don't talk, all his concentration on the rowing and mine on watching him carry me across to the other side.

From where we land on the other side of the lagoon the soil turns gradually to sand, a soft fine milky grey that rises to a mound and stops, a hood above the robe of beach that falls out toward the sea. "Here," Alvaro scoops up a handful of sand and shards. The shards are much like small stones, but flatter, the edges worn completely smooth. Some of them are striped with faded decoration, others plain, only distinguishable as pieces of pottery by their hand-shaped curves. He shows me some bone fragments too and a part of a skull, bigger than a dog's would be and rounder.

"Is this a sacred place?"

"This is the graveyard. Cuixmala, the graveyard," he says. "It means place where the bodies lie, place where the

175

souls rest."

"Doesn't anyone else come down here?"

"Not now, Antonio's family never lived here. They would come for holidays, for visits, sometimes to show the children. On Antonio's birthday we came once, when he was seven. They brought the ponies days before by boat, ponies so we children could ride, and servants to follow with cakes, and to carry everything. The day of the party we came in a plane. . . there was no road then. . . it was the first airplane I had ever been on and the pilot let me sit up where I could see. I loved that flying from the start. . .then Antonio's sister broke her toe, some of the children cried that the party stopped. . . it was a. . . confusion. . . is that the same word for you? . . .everyone excited. . . and I had to go back with the ponies and the servants on the boat."

"And were you sad?"

"Yes I was sad not to be on the airplane." He laughs. "You see how much I love my plane now, one of my own. If it was better I could show you everything."

"Did the children find the graveyard?"

"No. I found some. . . *fragmentos de ceramica*. . . bits of. . ."

"Pottery?"

"Some pottery. But I didn't tell." We are silent for a moment. I see him as a small boy stuffing pottery bits into his pockets. Then he smiles at me and takes my hand.

"Do you like my secret?"

"Yes, I like your secret."

We walk to the far end of the beach, as far as we can go before the trees start again, and sit on a log. The beach is very still. The air is still. Even the ghosts of the Indians are still unharassed by our presence, silent in their belonging to it. Except for some turtle marks and the three-pronged tracks of a dog, ours are the only footprints marking the

176

sand. There is no litter, no empty cans of beer, no ashes from campfires. Even the water looks untouched and clean. The blue of the sea stretches out forever, past my imagination. It is a place for lovers: the patina of day's-end light, the milk-grey sand, the soft warm air. Yet I cannot touch him; I cannot hold his hand; I can barely talk to him. My edges are like glass.

"At this place I could land new."

Before dinner Alvaro has a shower and changes his clothes. As I come into the house he stands at the doorway smiling, his arms stretched out as if to show me the special effort he has made. I am unprepared and awkward in my old jeans. We stand together, poised and ready, unable to move out of this frame and into the one that should follow. Mike calls us in to eat.

We have *huevos rancheros* and black beans at the big table. After we've finished and are drinking rum and teasing Mike about his night out—on paydays all the young men pile into the truck and drive to the nearest bar to drink and dance—three men stride in without knocking. Alvaro stiffens at their entrance but offers them drinks and chairs. Mike does not get up to greet them.

"*Hasta pronto*, Alvaro." Mike leaves.

"Joe Takanawa, Bob Barton, my lawyer. . . Alvaro Vasconcelos." The tall grey-haired man waves introductions and takes the best chair. "Got any whisky, Alvaro? No, okay I'll have the rum. Are you boys going to have the rum?"

"Oh I guess I'll have some of that rum you people like to drink here. How about a Dr. Pepper on the side?"

"Only Coca-Cola, sorry." Alvaro goes off to get the Coke. Takanawa starts on about Dr. Pepper. "If you could get these people to drink it, get a franchise in here, you'd have a goldmine. Best drink in the south now, outselling Coke."

The one who made the introductions lights my cigarette and asks me who I am. He looks surprised when I say I am a friend of Alvaro's, more surprised when I say I am staying at the ranch. "Here?" his voice barely veiling his disdain for the shabby walls, the bare floor, the ranch dog scratching under the table. The three of them look at me as though I am one of them gone wrong, a nice girl who fell off a bus tour and got mixed up with the wrong sort trying to get home. I get up and clear our dishes from the table.

They are Americans, I guess. They are all dressed in the cliché of American style: perma-press Bermuda shorts, freshly pressed sport shirts, expensive casual shoes. The one who hasn't said his name has the dissolute look of an aging son of a rich man, as Alvaro later says he is. He lives in a big house not far from the ranch because it is easier to live rich here than in the States. He doesn't bother to speak Spanish to Alvaro. I don't like them. They have come to talk business and when they leave, their conversation still hangs in the air like the cloying spray of pine deodorant. Everything real backs into corners; even the dog goes outside. Alvaro and I sit on the verandah to escape the sticky film of their dissemblance.

"Who are they?"

"Dehavilland, the tall man, was to buy a piece of land. He cheated on the deal. He came to make it okay, with his friends, with his lawyer, for support. I won't do business with him again."

"You were very polite to them."

"They came into my house."

"Why didn't he speak Spanish to you?"

"He never learned. Fifteen years he has lived here. His children speak some."

After a moment we talk about airplanes and ham radios and where we've been in the world. He doesn't have much time for the radio now, but in the early days, when he first came to work on the ranch, he would tune in almost every night to friends he never saw. A way to practise his English, but more. The airplane takes him to places; the radio found people in places the airplane couldn't go. Sometimes he would just listen and that would be enough.

Suddenly, he stands up and walks over to an alcove in the supporting wall of the side verandah and shows me the skull that is sitting there, a dull eye in the plaster wall. He found it in the graveyard ten years ago. I am wary of holding a thing so fragile and when he takes it down to give it to me I tense my hands into a cradle to receive it. For a minute I want to run my fingers around the inner rim of the eye holes but instead let it sit within the lattice bowl of my fingers. I give it a safe place. The skull is so much smaller than my head. When Alvaro takes it back his hands relax over its brittleness in a way mine cannot.

His voice is as soft as the air, then straining, tired of so much English. I try my Spanish for a while, but like candy that is pulled too hard the lines between us stretch, begin to break, my words too few and small to gather up the nuances of feeling I want to give back to him. I can't tell if what I sense is there, if he wants me or if I am only a foolish girl, drunk in a strange place. Perhaps I am only in love with Cuixmala. Perhaps what I feel from him that seems to be special is simply that wash of love that comes from those few people who are genuinely good. Antonio had said you will love Alvaro, everybody loves Alvaro, Alvaro will take care of you. I had almost seemed that I was a gift to him. It did not offend me though at other times I would have been outraged. There is nothing false about him and nothing cynical. A weariness, perhaps, and anger at men who cheat, but brightened with a boyish wonder and delight he must have brought as carefully into his adult life as the fragments from the graveyard. He hasn't tried to make me drunk; he's made no overt advances; he doesn't leer as his visitors leered. But he brought me down a coconut from high up in the tree, he rowed me across the lagoon, he changed his shirt, he shared his secret of the graveyard. Surely these signs are as potent as words. But without his words it's hard for me to find my own.

We talk for a long time in spite of the difficulties. It is comfortable where we sit; there is no light to pull the insects toward us. Down below the huts are quiet, the women and children asleep, the men still out drinking. The Great Danes, fallen asleep at our feet, stir occasionally, scratch, make smacking noises and roll back into sleep, comforted by our pats—each of us has kept a hand on a dog. We are facing each other in wide wooden chairs, sharing cigarettes and the ashtray on the arm of my chair. I notice that I have put my feet up on the bottom slats of his chair, and then, just as I am about to take them down—it is a familiar position for me, slouched back in my chair with my feet up, but here it somehow seems sloppy, uncouth—I realize that if he puts his hand on my bare feet, I'll be able to relax, perhaps place my hand on his hand, and from there it will be easy to go forward. So far we haven't really touched except when he helped me into the boat or steadied my hand to light my cigarette in the breeze. I wait for his touch now, wanting to say *"este bueno,"* it is good, the best I can convey in Spanish to mean yes, more than yes, I welcome you. He is telling me about his visit to London when I hadn't met him, only heard of Alvaro, you will love Alvaro, from Antonio and Cecilia who lived then in the flat below me. Why didn't I meet you then, Alvaro, would it have been easier in a place where we were both strangers, where there were no pictures of your family, of your tree that sprouted branches every year as far back as I was born, and there were no broken planes to remind you of birds that fall, that men grow old, that boldness and strength don't last forever, or would you have been shyer still, ill at ease in a fat coat worn against the cold. . . .

"It was so grey," he is saying, "the rain was not like here." Not like here, where it washes hard, and flowers, shaking off the wet, throw up a smell as strong and sweet as love come ripe. His hand is nowhere near my feet. They look so outrageously provocative, my painted toenails like red lights on a brothel street. I tuck them underneath me on the chair.

"You're cold." He puts his cigarettes in his shirt pocket. "We'll go inside."

Inside, he doesn't turn on the light but stops and asks me, "Where will you sleep?"

"Where would you like me to sleep?"

"With me, of course," but laughing, a joke. Why can't I say, "Yes, with you," instead of hesitating, grinding my confusion into manageable pulp, waiting too long to respond, so that he turns on the light and says, "Here, this room is best," and leads me toward the large back bedroom I haven't seen before.

We reach it through another bedroom, full of beds— two, three. . . five, I count, bare of covers except for one— and little else. A gunrack, a table, a chair, a hook near the door which holds a worn leather jacket, another near the made-up bed with two shirts on a hanger. Mike's work clothes thrown on the chair. No rug. Two small uncurtained windows near the ceiling. A framed photograph on the wall facing the door of a young man—Alvaro—beside a brand-new forties truck. I recognize the background, the shed behind the ranchhouse. "I will sleep here with Mike, there are lots of beds as you can see, and you will be safe in there." He draws back the cotton curtain that hangs across the doorway.

The room he leaves me in is long, like a sunporch covered in, with curtained windows along the outer wall and a door to the outside. There is a double-size iron bed near the inner door, painted a glossy brown and dressed with a white coverlet and plump white pillows that have embroidered edges on their slips. Beside the bed sits a plain wooden table covered with an embroidered cloth, on it a lamp, above the lamp Christ's body hangs stiff on its cross. The only carpet in the house lies on this floor, a pattern of birds with jagged tails and eyes still bright in spite of the fading pinks and greens. Like a child's mural but not quite, too playful, too happy bright. There are three pictures on the wall: one of cherubs holding a garland, tinted the same intense playroom colours of the rug; a black-and-white photograph of Alvaro's plane much like the one hanging by the beachhouse stairs; and a wedding photo. Grouped together at the far end of the room are a wardrobe, a dresser and a folding screen, the kind that provides a bit of privacy for dressing. The room is cared for, clean, not casual like the rest of the hacienda. Like a garden shaped from indurated clay.

I stare at the photo of Alvaro and his wife, at the groom's thick wavy hair and his wide smile, at the dark ingenuous eyes and the strong young body bound up in his wedding suit, at the bride's pretty plump face and her blond curls draped with white lace. The wedding picture seems to own the room, the objects and their arrangement part of the promise, the moment, the photo holds onto.

I find a chair behind the screen, undress, and fold my underwear on the chair with my jeans and blouse on top so nothing underneath will show, hiding my clothes the way I do before I have to lie on a doctor's examining table with my feet in the stirrups and my parts no longer private under the skimpy white sheet. Then I stuff my nakedness into the bed. I don't take up enough room; the bed feels empty. My nipples are covered with shiny silver flecks from the beach at Miramar that flash out to meet the light that filters through he doorway hanging. Is he asleep or just lying there, alert, as I am? Footsteps.

"Are you okay?" His voice from behind the curtain. "I'll be here in my sleeping bag if you need me."

Another phantom invitation, gone before I can catch it.

I lie there for a long time, not wanting, not able to sleep, waiting for something to happen, coaxing, pleading, begging my own courage to haul me out of bed and shove me naked into the doorway. Finally, I close my eyes and concentrate very hard to make his body materialize over me. Imagine his face, you know that, imagine his arms, you have seen them at least to the hems of his short sleeves, imagine his legs, still strong, feel the line of his neck, his back, move your hands over his ass and down around to his penis, which should be full now, ready to meet you, and then my hands shrink on the vast expanse of his stomach, his body's aging concentrated there, large, a weight falling on me, a beach ball, and I wonder if it will get in the way and lose him before I can come. I clutch my breasts and wonder if he has heard the bed creak. I listen for a long time. His light goes out, and so my body sags, struggles toward sleep, falls.

My dreams punch me around all night. A child in my care falls down a dark, endlessly deep well and I run through the plantation trees frantic for help. I run and run and find Alvaro by the graveyard, crying, he shakes me, you are not a woman, you did not make love to me, you are not a woman, and the dream is like the earth and we are its hot dark centre and I say I couldn't find the words, where were the words, and he says you did not make love to me.

In the morning when I come into the kitchen he has already taken the truck to the east side of the ranch to check the irrigation ditches and is standing slumped against the

183

counter, one hand under his head, the other pouring hot water into the coffee cups. He has buckled a broad, thick leather belt over his shirt. It suits him, gives him a samurai look of strength. But his eyes have the wounded look I remember from my dream.

"You look tired."

He stands up right away and hands me a cup, dismissing my remark. "I didn't sleep well. Some nights are bad. You must have them too sometimes, or you're too young perhaps," and looks at me with a kind of a smile. But he is more formal, more serious than the day before. He doesn't joke with me all day.

When it is time to leave we drive the long way round the ranch—I've asked him for a farewell tour—bumping over roads not meant for cars. I want desperately to have a truck to go exploring on my own farther than I could on foot. It is such an old land but so new to me. I want to touch Cuixmala and bring it closer to me. Maybe this intermingling of lush growth and dryness can teach me a fluency I don't have. I have visions of staying on the ranch forever, unrolling long, guttural Spanish phrases in and around its spaces, like ribbons the colours of bougainvillea. I feel immeasureably sad leaving it so soon, but when we close the last gate behind us I don't cry. My eyes are one-way mirrors.

We drive fast, not even stopping when we run out of cigarettes. Alvaro has business in Colima and his wife to visit; I have to find my way back to Mexico City in time to catch my plane home. At Manzanillo Alvaro makes some phone calls and I try to get a seat on the train. The doctor has told me not to fly. The daily train has left, which means I have to travel overnight by bus. In the meantime I have to go back to the beachhouse at Miramar and pick up my things. It is noon, Alvaro has an appointment in Colima at 2.00, my bus to Mexico City leaves at 8.00. We sit at a table

184

in the Zocalo and order two guava drinks.

"There is a buyer for the ranch." It is as though someone has struck us both.

"Why do they want to sell the ranch?" I am astounded, hurt.

"Oh. . . many reasons. I've known for a long time."

"And what about you, will you stay, what will you do?"

"I don't know. Maybe I'll stay, I don't know."

"Is it the Americans who came?"

"Not them, others the same."

It is harder to talk then. He looks so heavy.

"Drink up your guava juice, your Mexican drink, you won't have one in Canada," straining to joke again. "We'll drink to you," and touches his glass to mine.

"And to you, Alvaro, and to Cuixmala."

"Cuixmala."

The local bus to Miramar drives up on the other side of the square, people get off, I will have to get on. He hugs me hard and I kiss him, almost on his mouth, and run to get the bus before it leaves. By the time I pay my fare and find a seat the bus has heaved its way down the road and the Zocalo is gone.

I break the key trying to open the beachhouse door and have to get in through the sliding windows at the back that haven't been properly closed. Before I leave I write a note and set it on the mantelpiece:

Dear Alvaro,

I'm sorry I broke your key. I won't forget Cuixmala.

It takes me six tries to say that.

The sun is still bright on the beach. My towel so orange. How do I describe it, this brightness, this orange orange of cloth I am holding, its texture, how its folds form as I hold it, my feeling as I look at it, standing here on an empty beach, crying.

Even this old bus sails like a capsule through the night. Bits of Mexico seen through glass: a woman sits in the light of an open doorway, two boys in dusk-blue shirts jostle each other as they walk down the road. Unconnected phrases fill my head: *Donda esta el... Cuando volvera. Cuanto le debo.* Colima is more of a city than I expect. Before I change buses I go into the glare of the bus station to buy a *choco milck* for something to do. *Abra la puerta. Esto no functiona. Por donde. Donde me bajo, por favor?* When I get on the bus a middle-aged Mexican woman gets on, followed by a man and a boy who carry her bags. The man is curly-haired, blond, and speaks with an American accent. The little boy, in a straw beach hat, calls him Pop. They both embrace the woman warmly, a bit sad too. The man says, "Adios, Felicia." The boy says, "I'll write to you, Felicia," and she hugs him again. It is a long night's ride to Mexico City. The seats are too hard for sleeping.

At Peace

Ann Copeland

By sheer accident I happened to be passing through Saddleburg when the obituary columns listed Barney's death. Even
more accident that I happened to pick up a paper that night
and read of it. But for the CN breakdown, I'd have charged
right through that godforsaken burg and left it behind forever. As luck would have it, though, our ailing train gasped
to a halt about twenty miles outside town. After the usual
apologies, reassurances, official explanations and unofficial
speculations, they hauled us off, baggage and all, and left
us huffing and puffing in the frost, a band of about 50 de-
railed passengers thrust on the bleak bosom of a November
night in Maritime Canada. It was every bit as chilling as I
remembered it.

Small pockets of human frustration clustered alongside
the track, here and there a cigarette lighter briefly illumin-
ating anxious eyes or a stoic jaw, intermittent mutters use-
lessly rehearsing our impotence as we waited to be rescued.
The surge of rhythmic power that had so effortlessly borne
us past hamlets, shacks, straggling ends of villages, vacant
sagging barns, wintering maple and evergreen forests, miles
of unpeopled marsh, standing cows and scattered work-
horses—was still. For hours we had sat in the overheated
cars staring vaguely out at the darkening landscape that

passed us, lulled and rocked by the mechanical song of our train; or had we turned away from that mesmerizing window to the comforts of the inside: a drink, dinner, conversation, a snooze. But now our instinctive balances of cold observed and warmth enjoyed had been exploded. We were on the other side of that glass, we were out there, ourselves impossibly part of the desolate landscape with which we had felt so tenuously connected, if connected at all. *We* were in the moving picture, but we weren't even moving.

There was no inside to turn to, no way to shut this out, turn it off. The best distraction I could find from gradually numbing toes and buzzing irritation all round me was to stare straight up. I could remember that from before. It wasn't the old cliché of finding solace in the sky. Not that sky. It was simply that there was no sky like it anywhere else I'd been. There was nothing else to do with it but look. It was a sky that reduced one to staring. Going blank. A sky whose vast darkness somehow inverted and restated those vacant stretches of landscape it shrouded by day. Neither a pillar of fire nor a manned rocket seemed to have anything to do with those heavens. Stars were everywhere in the black, patterned holes cutting through—to what? No trace of that pinkish rainbow that arches over a large city at night, the almost sickening glow of darkness' covenant with urban hustle bustle. I can remember seeing, once, the night sky over the steel works in Gary, Indiana—puffed with swiftly merging forms of billowing grey-yellow above belching flames: gorgeous. Faced with that, one might come to believe in apocalypse. But this sky yielded nothing to human desires, it remained barren and silent even with studding stars and subtle wisps of whiteness graining through its black. I stared and felt again what I remembered feeling long before about the marsh sky: it was neither reassuring nor warming. It was silencing.

188

Eventually, as is usually the way with such human inconveniences, we were taken care of. They stuffed us all into a bus and transported us to a Holiday Inn just outside town from which they would collect us next morning and put us on the ten o'clock train they promised would leave promptly. When I finally lugged my loaded suitcase and parcels into that plastic world, even the blank surfaces of chartreuse and mauve in the predictable lobby and the equally opaque surface of the desk clerk were welcome. At times vacuity disguised as the familiar can seem to give warmth. This was such a time. I was relieved to be inside. In no time, I had squared away my belongings, freshened up, picked up a paper in the lobby and headed for the dining-room. One thing I remembered about Maritime food: their fish chowder was usually fabulous. This was the perfect night for a bowl of it.

When the waitress disappeared with my order I settled down with the paper. I'd had enough of enforced socializing and people-watching for that night, and soon enough I'd be back in my own nest of domestic wear and tear. For those few final hours, at least, I cherished my solitude. And so the unfailing defence: I folded back the evening paper and began to read.

By the time dessert came, I was to the obituary page. It didn't take long to reach the obits; papers in that section of the country are notoriously slim. And then, there it was:

Died

Sister Barnabas MacLean, 64, daughter of Angus and Genevieve MacLean of Scotland, coadjutrix sister of Order of St. Gertrude. Funeral from the Church of Our Saviour, Saturday, November 28. Friends may call at the convent between the hours of 3.00 and 5.00 and 7.00 and 9.00 on November 27. Donations may be made to the Heart Fund.

189

Barney, it had to be Barney. There could be only one lay sister in Maritime Canada named Sister Barnabas MacLean. Reading that notice seemed to paralyze all my responses momentarily. I didn't want Barney to be dead. Not, mind you, that I'd seen her in twenty or more years. But Barney had a corner in my consciousness that was carpeted, furnished, mythologized, and turned to in moments both secret and articulate. I had told many stories about her to dear friends. There were others I would tell no-one because she trusted me not to. There was a pact of secrecy and trust between Barney and me, had been since I left the Order and even well before that. Barney belonged to life, the life of memory and mind that was mine. I didn't want her buried.

I remembered our first encounter with a spasm of discomfort still. I was new to Our Saviour's community, fresh from the novitiate, impressionable, earnest and conscentious —not to say scrupulous about keeping untarnished and pure the vows I had just made. I realize now how hard it is to convey to an outsider what strange beings we were when we finally completed our three years of novitiate training and went to live in community. We were filled with ideals, many as yet untested, schooled to the observance of details we believed would become the measure of sanctity in a world that denied us more obvious martyrdom, committed to a daily round of prayer and meditation that was taxing, time-consuming and, we fervently hoped, eternally efficacious. Anyway, there I was, assigned that first year to help Sister Barnabas in the kitchen during my "free time"—of which there was none. (At using such euphemisms we all became unwittingly expert.) I had some vague notion that I was a victim. When I'd innocently told a few sisters what charge Reverend Mother had given me for the year, they rolled their eyes expressively, charity notwithstanding, and wished me luck.

So I found my way to the kitchen on my third day in the community. There she was, Sister Barnabas, puttering slowly around. It was ten o'clock in the morning, a Saturday.

"Good morning, Sister Barnabas," I said from the doorway, timid of crossing the premises without her clear sanction.

"Hrumph." It was barely audible. She kept moving about, grunting and sniffing, opening the refrigerator, shuffling to the sink, slamming cupboard doors, effectively communicating to me without so much as a word that she wished I was at the opposite end of the house, if not of the world.

"Reverend Mother told me I might be of some help to you in the kitchen."

She stopped dead. Then she looked at me, scowled and snorted. "Help! So that's her idea, is it? Never *has* liked the way I run this kitchen. So she sent a spy, eh?"

She slammed the drawer behind her with her broad rump and grabbed the broom. Sister Barnabas was lame. Like most people who have lived long years with a handicap, she compensated amazingly well. When she really wanted to move quickly, she did. Now she hobbled over to about two inches in front of me.

"Well, you can get right out of here and find yourself somethin' else to do to pass yer Saturday mornin's more in keepin' with the education the likes o' you has had." She started to sweep vigorously, covering my feet with the broom, forcing me back out of the doorway. "An' that's that!"

I left.

Something kept me from telling anyone about it. I held my peace and mentioned nothing to Reverend Mother. Not that at that point I wanted to conceal; it was some deeper instinct I couldn't name that said: let her be. So I did. But the next Saturday morning, promptly at ten, I appeared again in the doorway. This time I saw that the kitchen floor had been scrubbed and was glistening wet. Sister Barnabas was nowhere to be seen. It was understood that one didn't disturb her in her room, a tiny cell just across the hall from the kitchen. That week again I felt a bit guilty but decided nonetheless to leave her a note that I'd been there, let time pass, and try just once more the next Saturday.

At ten o'clock I appeared. There she was, hobbling about. Grumbling. Apparently oblivious that I was in the doorway. I waited. Then cleared my throat. She turned immediately, but it was clear that she was not about to help me.

"Good morning, Sister Barnabas."

She scowled at me once more. "Well, I got yer note." Not another word. No indication of how she felt. No explanation.

"Is there anything I could do to help you this morning, Sister?"

"Wash the floor." She pointed silently to the mop and pail she had left in the corner by the doorway. As she did that, she was loosening her apron, obviously not intending to be around while I helped.

"Fine." I held my tone as absolutely neutral as I could. Perhaps I did have a charge, after all.

She left and I moved about, sloshing the linoleum and hoping it would suit her. One thing worked in my favour: I knew she was not a fussy housekeeper. In fact, the prioress at that time kept away from the kitchen just because she couldn't stand the mess. The food Sister Barnabas fed us was excellent, the best in the province I later realized, after I'd moved around a bit. But the kitchen—a godawful mess. Pots within pots, nothing sized, jars and containers here and there with leftovers and promises dripping or hardening in various colours and shapes, a conglomeration only she could keep straight. Thick greasy dust coated the top of the refrigerator. The oven window was crusted with a baked glaze that resisted repeated applications of Easy-Off. I learned that later, when the oven came to be my special task, one I loathe even now.

And plants. Where there wasn't dirt or pots or pans or food, there was a plant. Counter space seemed to disappear almost before it existed. Ivy trailing all over the kitchen windows, even though the convent was poorly insulated the windows were frosty. A jade tree growing from a sodded wash basin in the corner, *impatiens* blooming fiery red on the edge of the butcher block in the centre of the kitchen, a tuberous begonia on the flour barrel, shifted about during the day as baking proceeded. And—who would believe it? —African violets thriving on the corner of the kitchen counter.

It made no sense; her plants were always in danger. But they were a precious part of her mess and she was scrupulous about their care. Talked to them, long before plant nuts were telling us that was the secret. Vented her spleen on them, too. Perhaps it was simply that she had no-one living with whom she felt she could communicate, so the plants got it—whole. And she had spleen aplenty. But they rooted and grew and flowered and trailed in that atmosphere of hostility and harangue. To this day I can't keep an ivy from dying, not even with the advantages of mild climate, peat moss, plant food, sun, water and a library of How-to books. All she did was mutter and growl, and this in a part of the world whose climate spoke of death. My milder skies of the Pacific northwest, the long growing season, the abundant rain—none of this has made my thumb green. But nothing green seemed to wither in Barney's kingdom.

Apparently my floor passed muster, for she let me in each

Saturday morning thereafter, usually muttering some direction to me and leaving immediately for her room. When I left the kitchen and headed down the hall an hour or so later, I'd often hear her cell door click as she shuffled back to inspect. We went on like this for some time.

Then one Saturday morning she paused as she was leaving the kitchen. She seemed to be making a more elaborate knot in the apron strings she was about to dangle from the hook behind the door.

"Sister," she grunted in my direction. I was busy pouring water into a pail and turned off the tap quickly to hear. "How come you never told Reverend Mother I wouldn't let you in my kitchen?"

"Because I figured you must have your own good reasons." The answer was true and it was uncalculated. As sometimes happens with such responses, unfortunately only sometimes, it went right to the mark. She didn't let on then.

"Hrumph." She hung up the apron and hobbled out.

The next Saturday, though, before I started my work, she offered a comment, as if a whole week hadn't intervened, as if we were just continuing our conversation. "Yer the first one has ever done that fer me here." She jabbed the apron onto the hook and left. I mopped away that morning with the distinct sense that in some queer way I'd made a difference in her feeling about the place, about me, or about I didn't know what.

I came to know what, of course, as months passed and our weekly punctuated exchanges grew into what couldn't properly be called conversations, ever, but limping dialogues that seemed to erupt, almost unwilled, out of some inexpressible need in her. For my part, I came to see certain things about Sister Barnabas.

First of all, somewhere, somehow, and it was probably many years before, she had been badly hurt. I was never sure just how. I could read the many subsequent hurts that resulted from her being the only lay sister in an Order of highly educated women, who willed to deal charitably with her but found it hard to absorb her thorns without the flower of articulate acknowledgment. For Sister Barnabas never admitted guilt. Nor did she speak easily or grammatically, nor even, sometimes, coherently. Before she could get a statement out, she had to feel she could trust you. Most of the time she made do with monosyllables and grunts delivered with a scowl. By the time I met her she trusted literally no-one. Except, for some strange reason as our history bore out, me.

Secondly, she was basically bright. She had had no schooling to speak of—just grades one and two in a little country schoolhouse. (I observed with fascination her self-taught methods of calculating proportions for enlarging recipes.) Then, when she was eight, she had lost both parents: first her father was killed in a freak accident by his own tractor, then her mother, a month later, died in childbirth. She was farmed out to a distant uncle who was none too happy to have another mouth to feed and body to clothe, but saw to it that she redeemed the burden on him by taking care of his four children, all younger than she.

She had known little about the sisters when she first came to them, had merely passed their convent whenever she went into the nearest town, some fifteen miles from her uncle's farm. As she grew older she occasionally saw them moving about in town and she understood—because she had her depths of uneducated piety—that they lived for God. She was about seventeen when her uncle told her one day that the sisters were looking for someone to help with the work in their convent. She took the hint, went timidly to investigate, and shortly thereafter went to live with the sisters. She had a place and she had a job.

"I felt I'd found a home," she put it to me simply, in one of her many narrations about life in the old days. "They needed an' wanted me. There wasn't many of them, but some very good souls. As well as one or two *divils*!" With this, she'd swat an imaginary fly or rub her hands energetically against her crusty apron for emphasis and relief, her dark eyes snapping beneath heavy disorderly brows. "But most of us got along real well. The superior fer years was Sister Alphonsus. She didn't put on airs." Here a pause with a meaningful sniff. "None o' this bowin' and scrapin' from here to eternity. We showed her proper respect but she was one of us. Did the dishes, taught in the classroom like the rest. No stayin' in her office, seein' people an' hearin' their reports on others from dawn to dusk." Again, she would italicize her complaint with a physical gesture—kick a box, slam a drawer, or perhaps, if we were chatting in her cell as later came to be our habit, she'd just slap her knee hard once or twice.

It was a particularly sore point with Barney while I was there that our prioress, as the superior was then called, was somewhat reserved and set great store by her dignity. She made no attempt to hide her disapproval of the way Barney kept, or didn't keep, her kitchen. She despised mess; her own office seemed dust-resistant, the top of her desk tediously neat. She and Barney lived in a state of cold war. But meals must go on: the *status quo* was maintained.

In any case, when Barney first went to live with the sisters in town, she found one substantial change in her lot: she felt valued. There was no great change in her material situation. As she herself put it, "We was all from that area an' most of us already knew what poor farm livin' was all about. So we worked hard an' didn't think much about it. Got mighty cold, tho', in mid-winter. That's what always bothered me most. *Cold.*"

Then the world began to change, even that world we may

think of as so unchanging. Their convent grew poorer and poorer. In the late twenties and thirties they were largely dependant on alms, their school income having dropped to virtually nothing. They skimped and prayed—and taught.

"We'd peel an orange for breakfast," she told me, "an' even that was an effort, our hands would be so cold. After breakfast I went around and started the woodstoves in the three classrooms so by the time the children arrived those rooms, the kitchen an' the little chapel would be warm." To me, her kitchen in Saddleburg was always stifling.

When Barney told them to me, I heard stories of those days with the fascination that attaches to some far distant era, for in my time we were snug in a convent that was spacious, orderly and well appointed if plain. In the fifties the superiors could afford to debate whether floors in a new convent would be hardwood or linoleum, whether the chapel would have a pipe organ or electric. But the times Barney spoke of were long before such affluence and the nuns in that little community came to know the meaning of the poverty they had vowed. Barney cooked for them as best she could, gradually mastering the secrets of the kitchen and the soil. Her hands, swollen with arthritis when I knew her, had the look of hands that were friends of earth.

"I'd always grown vegetables, even as a child," she boasted early one summer morning in Saddleburg, when she took me out behind our convent to admire her flourishing garden. "I surprised 'em àll when I managed to stock enough vegetables to take us clear through the winter."

Her secret was a method of storing in shallow holes out behind the convent, lined and covered with hay. It was on one of her early morning trips out to such a hole that she caught her foot in a crevice hidden by snow and turned her ankle badly. It never healed properly. She tried to keep the pain to herself; there was enough to worry about without doctors' bills. Somehow she hobbled about and managed to borrow first crutches, then a cane. When I came to know her in Saddleburg years later, she still had that same cane—horny worn smooth—the proverbial Irish walking stick.

Their little group managed to survive in that state for several years, perplexed as to their future but, one supposes, living day by day and pluckily trusting to Providence. I see them in my imagination as a small band of valiant women committed to the task of hanging on. They were receiving no subjects. Except for Sister Barnabas, as she came to be called, after she finally decided to become one of the group at the age of 26 or so.

"I wasn't sure they'd take me," she admitted to me in a rare show of humility once. "Especially since I couldn't help out in the school. Most of 'em had been through grade six at least. But they liked my cookin' an' they'd grown used to my ways. I felt right good they was so pleased to have me."

She always felt her lack of education. Even when I was in Saddleburg I'd come upon her furtively trying to improve herself. She kept a tattered pocket dictionary on a secret shelf and eventually she asked me to read and correct any notes she sent to Reverend Mother. For their communication was chiefly by notes, even though they lived in the same house.

So that was how she spent her early years in the convent. Her job was to scrape the pot as creatively as she could, but the bottom looked emptier and emptier. Their end seemed inevitable: gradual extinction. They were an autonomous house in the rural periphery of a particularly slack diocese. Times were hard all over and little help was forthcoming from ecclesiastical authorities who no doubt saw the hopelessness of wasting resources on a dying group.

Chance rescued them. I was on the other side of that

chance. But for the improbable, I would never have met Barney. As it turned out, my own Order—highly organized, international, strictly monastic as it was—reached out the sisterly hand. Officially it was called amalgamation. Perhaps interment would have been a more accurate term. Anyhow, Barney's little group of nuns was absorbed by us.

"No way we could know what we was in fer," she'd ruminate as she poked around the kitchen after our work was done, shifting the arbutus, checking the violets, or easing herself onto the rickety high stool near the sink. "But I'm tellin' you, Sister, I'm tellin' you—I never wants to live through seein' a house closed again. Not one I've been livin' in and thinkin' of as home. Not one I knows like the back of my hand and loves. It was awful, it was awful." Intense in memory for a moment, then she'd shuffle off, jostling herself back to present practicalities.

I could imagine the world she had left. It's the same today, only more so. This was an early version of the very scene I'd stared at for hours through the train window that later November night. But in her time the whole area was just *beginning* to depopulate, people moving away to greener pastures—which to Maritimers generally meant Upper Canada, if they could get that far. Somewhere they felt they'd have a chance. Farms—always a precarious source of livelihood in this rugged part of the country—were straggling into anonymous dereliction. The sagging grey barn was becoming a landmark everywhere. Wherever you turned there were signs of village life that once had been but now was gone: old vacant buildings with broken windows, abandoned tarpaper shacks, junked wagons, rusting car parts, mounds of debris, litter. Stragglers lingered on—the oldtimers who blended tobacco, tall stories and repetitive wit as they stood staring out at the vacant landscape; the lounging adolescents. But it was improbable that any am-

199

bitious school would stand a chance of success here. And our Order was committed to education.

"We gathered fer one final party in the old house," Barney told me. "Even the old students, many of 'em now grown with children of their own, came. I made a great cake —we all sang, then ended with Benediction together fer the last time. We had it outdoors, the chapel was too small fer the crowd. I'll never forget that final hymn, 'Holy God,' it was. Next mornin' they split us up an' shipped us out to the communities that had agreed to take us, by twos and threes. Sister Alphonsus and I came here. I wanted to bring my mutt, but they said NO." I thought of her kitten litter at the back door.

"Here" was Saddleburg, where the Order had a flourishing elementary school and was about to start the private girls' high school to which I was assigned. Thus—chance. There were about 25 in the community when she came. They desperately needed a cook; there were no lay sisters in this Order. The job was hers. They soon saw, I'm sure, that she had already developed her crotchets, but she was tolerated easily since the convent was large enough that they could leave her alone.

That was just it: they could leave her alone. From my perspective, Barney had come from a world one might almost call cosy: where convent and school were in one building, where in the midst of her morning a youngster from grade three might run into her kitchen to sneak a fresh doughnut, if their pungent odour had seeped down to the hallway toward the classrooms. Occasionally, even in their hardest days, Barney would prepare a treat for one of the primary grades and the children would greet her appearance at the classroom door with a cheer, for they knew it meant doughnuts, candy or the succulent candied cherries she turned out by the dozen at Christmas time. When she went to town, limping along with her perpetual frown, people nodded, or children darted up to her to introduce their parents. She was an institution. I'm not minimizing the hardships she must have known, but it was all within a context that had some human warmth for her. She knew where she fitted.

Now all that was gone. There was *no* going to town: these nuns were strictly cloistered. The school itself was an acre away. She saw the children only in the distance, lining up for classes or at recess time. They had never heard of her, much less smelled her doughnuts or tasted her candied cherries. Parents' Day was catered and held in the school; she never met the families. The convent itself was shaped like a Y: refectory and kitchen in one wing, chapel in another, nuns' cells and community room in the third. In chapel the nuns chanted Divine Office in Latin. To her it might as well have been Hindustani.

She fit in only one place: the kitchen. And that place was cut off from the others. Seculars were not allowed within the cloister; the sisters stayed away from the kitchen. So she was structurally cut off from the others, to say nothing of the fact that she had no history or training in common with the rest of us. Everyone in that order had at least a BA and, as the years passed and our training was upgraded, the younger nuns were sent on to graduate school. Sister Barnabas might have pronounced the same vows as we had, but in everyday living that language of shared aspiration was a delusion. All the tongues we spoke in the course of a day were to her foreign, even threatening: it was a living babel called community life.

Just about that time I came to the house and went through my Saturday morning trial period before gradual acceptance came. Just why it came was never clear to me. Maybe not to her. Perhaps it was just that conjunction of person, need and time in one's life that worked, as it sometimes can, for the most unlikely reasons.

"Sister," she'd say to me as I was about to leave on Saturday morning, "do you have a minute?" I dared not say I was rushed, had to prepare a class, had papers to do. Instead we'd go across the hall to her small cell, the only one in that wing. Outside—the silent polished corridors, glistening formica-topped tables in the long refectory, the spotless community room, the tidy cells of the older nuns. Everywhere the house reflected order, an order understood to mirror timeless higher realities. Inside Sister Barnabas' room—clutter, glorious clutter. I understood why she never let anyone in.

First of all, the bed had on it no standard white cotton spread of the kind that reduced our cells to facelessness. Her bed was covered with an old quilt carefully patched in places.

"A variation on the Dresden plate," she told me, patting it with her swollen hands and then plopping down in the middle of it as she motioned me to the one small chair.

"In the old days we spent winter evenin's workin' quilts with pieces o' cotton the parishoners brought us. Turned out 'bout two a winter, mostly local favourites: Dresden plate, the bear's paw, double Irish chain, Maltese cross. They brought patterns with 'em from their families." ("Patterens" she said, I can still remember.)

Her words conjured up a homey rural scene to my stereotyping imagination: a group of nuns gathered around the quilting frame by the Franklin stove. Snow outside. Currier and Ives in the Maritimes. No doubt there was tedium in it, I thought, but there must have been steady delight, as well, in working with such beautiful designs and colours. Once a year, for their bazaar, they always raffled one or two quilts.

"One year Orville Landry took a chance in my name," she

gleamed. "He was our jack-of-all-trades, a handyman. Loved my cookin'. I used to send him home with a batch o' fresh doughnuts every Saturday night. Anyhow, didn't he win the quilt and give it to me."

It may sound like a trifle but just such a detail represented the gulf between these two worlds: her old convent world and the one she and I were now in, the only model I had known, in fact until I met Barney. For we, trained—with some pride, I always felt—to revere the austerities of monastic observance, had eliminated colour from the mind's horizon. And gifts. Whatever we received we turned in to the superior, and we soon learned to warn family and friends not to give anything that was colourful. I can still remember the gaily-striped towels I brought with me to the novitiate. On my second day there they disappeared and were quietly replaced by thin white ones. Towels in the convent were white, bedspreads were white, nightgowns were white, one is tempted to say now that the mind went white. The possibility of snuggling down under a colourful quilt that was your very own, a gift from someone you knew, was simply anathema to our highly conditioned virginal imaginations.

The abundance of things to look at in her room! Tacked to her walls was a hodge-podge of fraying snapshots, all from the past: squinting, squatting youngsters crowded together in a photo that was all background and taken on the slant; an aging tintype glued to cardboard backing of a broad-bosomed woman sitting sternly in front of her little cottage.

"My grandmother," she told me, "on my mother's side."

A dog, several shots of the dog, the cheerful mutt who had his own warm spot next to the wood stove in the kitchen of the old house. Her walls were covered with these photos larded in between with holy cards of the saints: St. Teresa of Avila in ecstasy; St. Joseph holding a lamb and a staff; the Child Jesus, heart and halo glowing; Mary, decorous in blue and white, grinding the serpent; Blessed Mary Alacoque receiving the promises; and, of course, the children of Fatima. The small table by her bed held a plastic madonna that lighted up in the dark. Sister Barnabas couldn't stand the modern austere decor of our new chapel. She loved plaster statues, vigil lights, tabernacles decorated in gold leaf with little doors that opened, processions with strewers, the Lourdes hymn: that whole disappearing world of comforting Catholicism we had been trained to regard as theologically and aesthetically suspect. She hated the revised liturgy. Having mastered, with great pride, the Latin responses at Mass, she had no interest in reverting from *Et cum spiritu tuo* to "And with you, too." Her thumbworn *Imitation of Christ* was there on the desk, next to the piled-high travel magazines the milkman brought her.

That first day, my initiation into her world of clutter and comfort brought me a feeling of release tinged with guilt: guilt because we chattered away in her cell, which was forbidden by the rule of silence, guilt because we stood in a world full of clips from the past and I had been trained to let that past go, to forget, or suppress, or sublimate—whatever word a more sophisticated secular analyst might apply —the strands that had brought us to where we were. Leaving home had meant to me *leaving* home: "He who having once put his hand to the plough looketh back. . ." We accepted, with some perverse pride, the cold absolute that we never would see home again. "Not even if there is a death in the family." That was the way they put it to us. Such a peak of detachment from home represented to us an achievement.

Yet there we stood surrounded, held, and (I felt it consciously even then) warmed by colourful fraying strands from a past of hardship that were gathered as best they could be into a whole skein of life: the effort to hold what had spoken, warmed and comforted in a world that was obviously now for Sister Barnabas cold, austere and fundamentally incomprehensible. I began to understand the litter of her kitchen; I began not to see litter so much as composition, to grasp why she worked so hard at each original piece she produced.

For that too was special about Barney. She had in her a touch of the artist. It showed in a variety of unexpected turns: she baked gorgeous, extravagant birthday cakes, quite unasked, and sent them into the refectory on the appropriate day for Sister So-and-so. The prioress disapproved visibly (we were not to celebrate birthdays but baptismal days) but found it futile to argue. I was assigned to keep track of the birthdays, to discover them by some means and let her know. She usually got a thank-you. She was wounded to the quick if she didn't though she'd never let on to the sister in question.

When I came into the kitchen one Saturday morning, I found her muttering and kicking an empty carton about fiercely. I waited a moment, wondering whether I ought just to leave (she valued her privacy passionately), then said as if I'd noticed nothing: "Anything special for me to do today?"

She booted the carton a good six feet till it struck a wall and, turning, slammed in an offensive drawer.

"Think all that matters round here is sayin' your prayers, doin' your work. Can't tell me God Hisself don't like birthday cakes!"

She had just received a note from Reverend Mother urging that she at least adopt more religious motifs for her cakes, not the usual dogs, cats, houses, flowers, et cetera. The one the evening before had been particularly offensive, it seemed. So Sister Barnabas growled and kicked and scowled her way through the next 24 hours, simmering with resentment. The next sister to be so honoured got a cake with a bleeding heart on it.

She made her own Christmas cards. I don't think Reverend Mother ever knew. It was quite possible that she didn't, for Sister Barnabas, down there in her wing of the convent, had her own world. She kept kittens out near the back door and her Christmas cards were rough drawings of a kitten or two with a red ribbon, coloured not painted, and a conventional little message written inside. These she started to put together in her spare hours sometime in October, and she would give them to the milkman, the deliveryman, the breadman, the garbage collector, the string of people who came to her back door during the year. I liked to think of the circuit of relationships that emanated from Sister Barnabas' back door: a network of people who spoke her language and read her scowls, were not put off, brought her little treats and favours which she never turned in but hoarded in her cell. She had her favourites and she played them. What I got from her treasure-hoard on my birthday was positively embarrassing but there was no getting around it.

It is extremely difficult to try to recreate now the texture of our relationship during those three years I spent at Saddleburg. It settled into a kind of tacit complicity, for she simply disregarded impossible restrictions she couldn't see the sense of, and went her way. I was a different breed; I had to balance two kinds of consciousness. Trained to much more rigid ideals, I had my twinges. But through it all, Sister Barnabas' obdurateness, her persistent passionate grasp at the bits of life she could still hold, her rage at what had been lost and her inability to say what—for in some ways she had never even known what, she could only feel its loss—these realities touched me more deeply than the hours of teaching, of living with that community, of doing what was expected and trying to fathom its meaning.

When I left Saddleburg, having been transferred to another house several hundred miles away, Sister Barnabas wept. She did it in the privacy of her room; she was nowhere in evidence the next morning when I left officially, the whole community standing around outside the front door to say the prayers for travellers and then good-bye.

At supper the night before, she sent me a note by the server, scrawled on the back of an envelope in her childish hand:

Come see me after nite prayer.
                    B.

There was no denying it. Great Silence or not, she would have her private farewell.

So, after night prayer, when the others were padding off to study hour or to get ready for bed, I went to Sister Barnabas' cell and knocked.

"Sister?" a whisper from behind her door.

"It's me."

She opened the door. Inside seemed strangely dim and shadowy. Then I saw what she had done. The cluttered little cell was aglow with dozens of candle stubs, sacristy butts no doubt, lighted and stuck anywhere she could perch them. I suppressed my instant urge to warn against fire: the holy cards, photos, papers, old magazines seemed to be leaping toward the flames, in my excited imagination. She took my hand and pulled me inside.

Sister Barnabas (Barney I called her to myself even then) had prepared a party for me. Her own kind of party. It was like a child's birthday party. Red, pink and purple balloons hovered up against the ceiling. Flickering candles cast huge blobs of dancing shadows on her white walls. The house outside her room was absolutely still. She had her small transistor radio that the garbageman had given her three Christmases before going softly on FM. By some miraculous effort, she had cleared her desk and set on it a masterpiece. On the cake, built high above the top layer, stood a replica of the convent we were in. A light on in one window, the kitchen. And underneath the replica, "Good-bye." Sister Barnabas was almost speechless herself at the effect of her efforts on me.

That passed quickly, however, and we settled down to cake and coke. I asked no questions. She had her ways. Her gesture made me want to cry, but I didn't. There was some steel impulse in me that said, "Hold on, it will be too much." It would have been. Instead, we gorged ourselves on Barney's seven-layer cake. She had wrapped several small presents for me and I was expected to open these, one by one.

"Do you like it?" she asked with childlike eagerness as I'd barely finished opening the can of Johnson's Baby Powder. Then the new toothbrush. Then a little box of Christmas cards she had saved for me. And the most touching perhaps, a bookmark for my Office book: the cut-out head of the Virgin pasted on a small strip of leather she had found somewhere and trimmed with pinking shears. I have it still.

Our party lasted about an hour. That was all the time I could manage, with packing yet to finish. But Barney had made her point. At the door to her cell she hugged me and bristled her black whiskers against my cheek, then turned brusquely back into her cell hiding tears.

Life has a way of simply going on. The large hurdles like goodbyes are risen to and then gradually fade before the onslaught of daily tasks, deadlines and expectations to be met in the ordinary business of getting through 24 hours. It was the same in the convent, only perhaps more so for us for we never had those upholstered pauses I now recognize as part of a normal rhythm of day-to-day living "outside": the evening when you choose to forget the outer world and curl up before the fire once the children are in bed, the latch is on the door, and the tentacles of encroaching minutiae are temporarily at bay. In the convent as I knew it, there were no such pauses. We moved from task to task, recreation itself was a task, staying awake in chapel could be a task, trusting the validity of one's own responses became a task—especially when they were at variance with what was expected. Days passed. Years passed. We worked. We prayed. We did our best to survive intact.

Through those years during which I moved about from house to house I never once heard from Barney. Of her I would hear periodically, just enough—usually conveyed in guardedly judgmental words—to convince me that her life went on as I had known it, fringed with dust and decaying strands, built on the bits of human contact she could elicit in an environment that was basically hostile to her. And to which she herself was hostile. Now and then a friend who had spent time at Our Saviour's would mention some anecdote about Barney. I gleaned that she was still cooking creations for birthdays, that her kitchen was still messy beyond description, that she was still so grouchy the prioress found it virtually impossible to assign anyone to help her—that she was still, that is, herself as life had made her.

Five years passed before I decided to leave the Order for good. That is not part of this story really, except that my leavetaking made possible our final meeting. I left, moved far away, worked, eventually married. The shape and feeling of different periods of our lives is mysterious. I passed through several phases of feeling about that chunk of my life, but ultimately came to hold it all at a distance. It ceased to be as living or as painful as it once had been, before the growing realities of husband, family, time passing, grey hairs, and all that whispers to us that regrets are a waste of time. Still, somewhere quite alive in my fading memory of detail there was a short, stumpy, grouchy, affectionate face and figure: Barney.

I didn't know how living that figure was until her letter came. The first one arrived shortly after my second baby was born. We were still in the welter of two sets of diapers, sibling jealousy, and house clutter that says life has exploded in colossal disregard for tidiness and order. It was fitting that into this world of fraying nerves and sharp edges muted by the welcome of loving affection that underlay our fatigue, Barney's letter came. She would have understood and responded to the mess. I remember sitting down in the midst of unfolded diapers, a mountain of them, while Jeffrey finally settled into play-dough and the baby was building up for a good yell. I wanted to indulge immediately the unexpected surge of feeling that had risen at this sudden link with a world that had seemed so far-off. I hadn't known I would be so glad to hear. I had spoken often of Barney, and with affection. But I had *placed* her in my imagination; her spot was fixed in my memory. Now she was dislodging herself, refusing to be put away neatly, asserting her living right to be as she wanted to be.

Dear One, it read. I had to struggle to make out that childish scrawl, large letters on small pages of what looked like her own card, a kitten on the front. *I have not forgot u. u no I did luv u. Life hear is worse than it was tho I no u suffered. i did see it even tho i never sed so. i no u have a good husband now and a baby.* She had not heard of the recent addition. *i want u to no i still think of u. if i cud i wud send u sweets. think of me.   B.*

Then began our correspondence. It had the same character as our old Saturday morning eruptions had had. I tried to write regularly over the next four years despite our many moves, our growing family, and my own work. She had awakened some sense of loyalty that I wanted to keep alive. Her notes came spasmodically, almost as if some moment in her life that laid claim on her with a particular stranglehold forced her to choke out a letter to a far-away friend. One came, two years ago now, which read in part: *u no, dear one, that if i cud, i wud have left myself. but where wud i go?*

It saddened me. Where would she go? She could never at this point—for she was well over 60, I thought—go anywhere. And she suffered so there. That was clear from her notes, almost illegible and illiterate as they were.

Then this. "Sister Barnabas MacLean."

There was something offensive and compelling in it. I had had no plan ever to revisit that convent. I had been going to pass right through Saddleburg with no train stop at all that night because I was at the tail end of my journey, at that point of fatigue that leaves the traveller with only one desire: to get back to the warm comforts of home. I still had a distance to go. At Montreal Tom would meet me and we would fly from there back to Vancouver to collect the children from grandparents before heading home. Home. Somehow, sitting over the last of the chocolate sundae in the Holiday Inn that night in November, I wanted desperately to be back home, fast.

But first this. Barney. I reread the notice several times. There was no way around it. If I chose to, thanks to the breakdown of the good old CN, I could see Barney for one last time. If I chose to. That was the hitch. There wasn't likely to be anyone there that I knew except Barney. What kept me sitting over the second and then the third cup of coffee that night was not any fear that familiar faces would awaken old discomforts, it was simply the question of whether I wanted to see Barney that way.

But there was something else that stirred me, that finally made me gather up the check and head for the room to ready myself and call a cab. It wasn't quite the banality of paying one's last respects but, to be honest, it had something of that in it. Mixed with the need, perhaps, to confirm in my own sensibilities the fact that Barney was dead. My going had something to do with her and something to do with me. For her it seemed somehow right, foolish as it is to suppose our visits of final deference have a thing to do with the dead themselves. But what exactly was that feeling? That someone coming, someone from the outside who had known her on the inside, who had understood her own alienation and perhaps re-enacted it in another way, that my coming was—what is the word—"fitting"? Right. Somehow a circle come complete. For me the meaning was clear. It cut a continuity. Not at all a physical continuity like the loss of a child or a parent. A spiritual continuity. That point of common understanding in this world was gone. Just that. Gone. I had to be sure. And honour its reality.

So I went. The taxi was about five minutes late, time enough for me to stand in front of the Holiday Inn stamping my feet as I tensed myself against that November air, time enough to lose myself for a few moments in that resplendent sky. There really is nothing like it elsewhere: of that I'm convinced. By day the scenery there would have to be called bleak: the long low marshes, few sloping hills, forests of evergreens, stubby farmlands, grey barns—a littered landscape of indigence and lack of imagination. But by night that disappears. It was years—21 to be exact—since I had felt my neck grow stiff as I strained to follow this design, then that, in the fluffing Milky Way. Orion. The Big Dipper. A night world of pattern revealed by depthless black. The world above. Barney up there?

The taxi came and I slammed in, gathering my inner forces for this last visit. It had about it that character and I was sensitive to it. How often in this life was I likely to find myself alone, travelling, away from family and friends, driving through a landscape that once had held me, revisiting it almost as if I were someone else? It was a privileged moment. I felt that.

I asked the taxi driver to wait. The convent was the same. I could just make out the familiar dimensions in the darkness: the heavy front door, the wing with the cells and the community room in it to the left, the chapel wing to the right. Extending out back, invisible from the front, would be Barney's wing, the kitchen. Who, I wondered, took over?

"Good evening." The sister was politely inquiring as she opened the door and held it ajar for me to explain myself. She was middle-aged, rather nondescript. Her face had that blond look that ages poorly, pale shading into paler. Her modernized habit was unflattering.

"Good evening. I've come to pay my respects to Sister Barnabas." I didn't even stumble over the formula. It came with the mechanicalness that gets us through some of life's worse moments. I was caught up in a sensation I hadn't expected: utter familiarity. For one brief instant I had the urge to say to the sister: *And if you'll just stand aside, I'll find my way to her cell and the kitchen.* But I didn't. I behaved. There was something indescribably strange in that moment of unintended masquerade. Strange—and comic.

"Come in." She smiled faintly, then turned wordlessly as I shut the door behind me and, ignoring the heavy inner doors that read CLOISTER, led me through another door to the right into a small parlour. Of course. I had forgotten that. They would wake her in one of the outside rooms so the public could come. *The public.* The garbageman? The milkman? I wondered who had come. That barrier of inside outside had been so thoroughly obscured in my mind that it was a momentary shock to come smack up against it. The Cloister Door. I had lived on the other side of that. But here, Barney and I re-met on the outside. Had we been there all along?

There was no-one in the visitor's parlour except the casket with Barney in it and one nun praying. This I dreaded. I hate corpses. I hate going to look. Why on earth this compulsion to see Barney again? Then, steeling inner responses, I walked over and knelt automatically at the prie-dieu before her.

It wasn't Barney. Of course it was, but it wasn't Barney. She was in the habit, hands folded, rosary through them. I had never seen her look neat. Her headdress was straight. Her whiskers were gone. Whoever prepared the corpse had shaven the chin smooth, removing one of Barney's most characteristic marks. She was smiling—that pasty, waxen smile meant to reassure us that wherever she was things weren't that bad. I had never seen that smile on Barney. Her forehead was smooth. No scowl. She lay in a simple box, as was the custom, with a white lining. There were no flowers. Those I didn't miss. But I wanted ivy, arbutus, philodendron, African violets, *impatiens*—the plant that always seemed to fit Barney. I wanted them all there, surrounding her indiscriminately. I wanted the scowl. Maybe a big cake on the casket saying "Goodbye" with a kitten on the top. Something colourful. The quilt as a lining for the casket. I didn't want this effigy of nunhood, of dedication and service. I wanted the real thing: screaming dissonances in that sterile setting.

Nowhere could I find it. I could imagine her kitchen.

Someone would have cleaned it already. Of her room I hated to think. What had happened to the bosomy lady in front of her cottage? Was the plastic madonna already at the dump? The nun behind me went on praying. The silence was oppressive. A tall beeswax taper at the end of the bier sent flickers of shadow across the still form. It wasn't Barney.

I nodded to the sister and headed for the door. There, Sister Poker-face was waiting for me and she noiselessly opened the outer door. I could see the exhaust from the taxi billowing pale grey in the darkness. He had kept the engine idling against the cold.

"Thank you for coming. She is at peace."

I nodded. I wanted to rage. I wanted to scream: "You don't know me, but I know you. You didn't know Barney, but I knew her!" What was the point? There was no way. Could any scream penetrate it?

As I walked down the path I heard the heavy door click behind me. Then, one look up. I was grateful for the cold air. And stars. The vast Milky Way. The sky that turned all this dark and illumined its own shuddering spaces with something not warm but clear. Cold. It cleansed. I breathed deep and looked for a long moment. Goodbye sky. Then I heard the motor revving. The cabbie leaned over and opened my door.

At first in halting spasms, then with that satisfying surge of power that says all connections have been made, our engine built up to a steady rhythm. Spent, I leaned back against the seat and closed my eyes, grateful to be borne away in the dark.

WILLIAM PATRICK KINSELLA is from Edmonton. His short stories have appeared in a wide variety of Canadian magazines. He is currently teaching fiction and working toward an MFA in English at the Iowa Writers' Workshop. A collection of seventeen stories, all told by Silas Ermineskin, the narrator of "Illianna Comes Home," and titled *Dance Me Outside* was published by Oberon earlier this year.

W. D. VALGARDSON is the author of *Bloodflowers*, *God Is Not a Fish Inspector* and *In the Gutting Shed*. His work has appeared in *Best American Short Stories* and he has been the recipient of the University of Western Ontario President's Medal for fiction. At present teaching in the department of Creative Writing in Victoria.

BETH HARVOR was born in New Brunswick in 1936. She now lives in Ottawa. She is the author of a story collection *Women & Children* and is presently working on two books —a novel entitled *Anatomy, Destiny* and a book of stories entitled *The Sunday After the War*.

JACK HODGINS teaches in a high school in Nanaimo and is the author of a story collection *Spit Delaney's Island*. A novel entitled *The Invention of the World* was published in 1977. His stories have appeared in magazines in the USA, Australia and Canada.

ELIZABETH SPENCER has now lived for many years in Montreal. Her last book was entitled *Ship Island and Other Stories*. Her best known novel is *Light in the Piazza*.

KENT THOMPSON lives and teaches in Fredericton. He is the author of two novels, *The Tenants Were Corrie and Tennie* and *Across From the Floral Park*. His stories have been published in many magazines and have been widely anthologized.

JUDITH PENNER was born in 1945 and grew up in British Columbia. She has worked at a wide variety of journalistic jobs in Canada and in London including a stint for the *Observer*. She is now living in Nova Scotia working on fiction. This is her first published story.

ANN COPELAND lives in New Brunswick. Her work has appeared in the *Texas Quarterly*, *Western Humanities Review* and *Canadian Fiction Magazine* where her story "Siblings" won the 1975 Contributor's Prize. "At Peace" will be published in Martha Foley's *Best American Stories of 1977*. She is at present working on a series of short stories about religious life.

ISBN 0 88750 237 7 (hardcover)
ISBN 0 88750 238 5 (softcover)
ISSN 0316-7518

Cover: Jane Martin. Design: Michael Macklem

Printed in Canada

PUBLISHED IN CANADA BY OBERON PRESS